ODD MAN OUTLAW

ODD MAN OUTLAW

BY

K.M. ZAHRT

WordCrafts

Published by WordCrafts Press
Tullahoma, TN 37388
www.wordcrafts.net

For Katie

Opening Statement

To *The Grand Rapids Times* and concerned citizens:

Eddie Waters was not and is not a criminal. Yes, everything that happened to him was his fault, to some extent, as a result of poor judgment, but to blame him solely would be an oversimplification. Countless rumors have been circulated in regards to Waters' case. Some people have said Eddie Waters was a deviant, a rebel, a bad seed. Others have said he was simply mischievous. Others still have said Eddie Waters was bound to be a failure; he was a drain on society, a thorn in everyone's side from the very beginning, and they always "knew it would be so." A few folks have even taken it a step further and proclaimed Eddie Waters was something more; they have said he was supernaturally evil, demon-possessed, perhaps even partly the devil himself. But all of these conclusions have been reached hastily, for Eddie Waters' case has not yet been heard.

It is possible Eddie Waters was delinquent by nature. He was foolish - I will grant that - and he was naïve, no doubt. But, for that, who among us could not be condemned? Who among us has not, unwittingly, made mistakes? Who among us has not, even with fair warning, made poor decisions?

A parent says to a child, "Be careful. The fire is hot." But how many children do not learn their lesson until it's too late, until a burned finger instinctively retreats? Only then does a child become cautious around heat. And how is such a child handled? The parent begrudgingly says, "Now, you've learned your lesson." Obviously, it would have been better for the child to heed the warning in the first place. Even so, the self-inflicted wound is punishment enough. Therefore, in naiveté lies not only the problem, but also the solution: forgiveness.

I believe Eddie was a victim. He was a victim not only of a manipulative individual in Norma Baker, but also of a culture of ignorance, a culture blinded by fantasies and fallacies. Lies, big and small, are told every day to "rationalize" reality, but those lies are dangerous, even more dangerous than the reality those lies intend to hide. A culture so manipulated by rhetoric and massaged by propaganda cannot see reality, can it?

It seems everyone believes they are entitled to their interpretation of the Waters' case, but most of those opinions are formed from misinformation. Some lack evidence all together. As Eddie's best friend, and as someone who is privy to the true details, it is my duty to set the record straight. Once Eddie's side of the story has been told, an informed discussion can resume, and then you may decide for yourself whether or not Eddie Waters is guilty of any crimes.

At that point, if you choose not to consider all the angles - if you choose, rather, to disregard this, satisfied with your ignorance - important questions must be asked. For the *Times*, what would happen to your credibility, your code of ethics and your responsibility to the public? I understand that this will, most likely, be discarded without a second glance or even a hint of guilt. After all, who would be responsible for such negligence? Would it be the staffer that receives this? No. That would not be fair. You, staffer, do not get paid enough for that. So, staffer, be sure to pass this on to your supervisor in order to keep your own hands clean, because you'd be surprised what you may be held accountable for someday. If you don't believe me, ask Eddie.

And for you, general citizen, if this reaches you, how would you be any less guilty than Eddie Waters if you disregard information that is at your disposal? Please remember one thing: Eddie Waters did not get a fair warning. He did not have the opportunity to evaluate the reality of his circumstances and to make an informed, thoughtful decision. He was in troubled waters.

Finally, the purpose of this is not, as some might speculate, an attempt to exonerate Eddie Waters of the charges against him for aiding Norma Baker. That is, after all, what he did. It's an attempt to correct the public's misunderstandings of what Eddie *thought* he was doing. The following is a collection of firsthand accounts, either mine or others from those close to Eddie during the period in question. All the details, events and conversations repeated here are - either factually or conceptually - done so with the utmost regard for truth and integrity, to the best of my ability.

I would like to thank everyone who cooperated with my investigation, whose full names have been changed and/or withheld for their protection, particularly those labeled as Maria, Brad, Eva, Sam, David and Shirley. I have set down these accounts in direct contrast to the profligate accounts promoted in the media to offer you a fair chance to evaluate both sides of the story and to maintain my own credibility - a virtue to which the media appears to lack all subscription. Thank you in advance to those of you who give this the attention it deserves.

Sincerely,
Citizen "Cid" Goodman

THE GRAND RAPIDS TIMES
Escapee Baffles Local Police
Authorities Fumble Investigation

In a statement to the press, Grand Rapids Police confirmed that Norma Baker, twenty-four, escaped from the Fifth Street Women's Correctional Facility (WCF) in downtown Grand Rapids. Baker escaped several weeks ago through a tunnel found in the prison's pantry where she was on a work assignment. Authorities claimed to have kept information about Baker's escape confidential in order to prevent public-wide panic. Sources confirmed the statement, adding, "We consider Baker to be harmless."

Baker was convicted of murdering her stepfather, Gene Mortenson, in Jigsaw, Michigan, in 2000. Mortenson was a well-respected attorney, and the community was deeply saddened by the loss. Throughout the trial, Baker maintained that she acted in self-defense, suggesting Mortenson was sexually abusive. She served seven years at WCF before escaping in mid-June.

After an extensive search, detectives were unable to apprehend the fugitive. The Police Department is now the subject of scrutiny. According to authorities, an internal investigation is underway to determine whether or not the department followed protocol.

Anyone with information regarding the whereabouts of Norma Baker is asked to contact the Grand Rapids Police Department immediately.

Exhibit One: Education

I met Eddie Waters on the first day of college. It was late afternoon by the time I arrived at what would be our dorm room. I found him passed out in a desk chair, drooling all over, with a book opened flat on his belly. He was there alone. He drove himself to school, car packed to the hilt. And there I was with my parents and twin sisters in tow, arguing and carrying on. Eddie told me he'd been there since the early morning. I asked him why all of his belongings were stacked to the ceiling on one side of the room. He said he thought he'd wait until I got there to decide how to make arrangements. He was thoughtful and caring like that.

During orientation week, before classes started, Eddie and I were hanging out in our room watching a rom-com starring Ben Stiller and Jennifer Aniston when we heard two girls talking in the hallway.

I nudged Eddie with my elbow, nodding toward the door.

"Don't," he said.

"You're good for me," I said. The girls walked passed our doorway before I could assess them. "Did you recognize them?"

"I wasn't looking," Eddie said.

"Hello," I shouted toward the door.

"Stop it, Cid."

"How you doing?"

Eddie slapped his palm to his forehead and shook his head.

"What?" A female voice rang throughout the room. It gave me such a start, I almost fell out of my chair. The girl now standing in the doorway looked like Sporty

Spice. She was wearing running shoes, athletic pants, and a blue sports bra that could be seen through her form-fit white t-shirt. Her tight abs were perceptible through her shirt as well. She was cute, too, with rounded cheeks and sandy brown hair tied back in a ponytail. Her fists were planted on her lean hips, elbows facing out - the commanding posture of one about to make demands. Her blue eyes sparkled as she smiled.

"What do you want?" said Sporty Spice. I wanted to retreat. It was safe to assume she'd kicked a few guys' asses before, but it was too late. "I wanted to ask you a question," I said.

"You're such an idiot," Eddie said to himself.

"What?" said Sporty Spice.

"Yes, Cid, what?" Eddie added. "This'll be good, I'm sure."

"Does your boyfriend go to school here too?" I couldn't help it. All of the things I could think to say were either pick-up lines or dirty jokes. I went with a pick-up line.

"Oh. My. God." Sporty Spice's friend, who had been standing out of sight in the hallway, pushed her way into the room. The friend was voluptuous, but in a lean way. She was wearing a skin-tight black tank top and khaki short-shorts. Her apparel showed all of her curves - taut and tanned legs to shapely hips to in-your-face breasts. Her hair was long and dark, elongating her round - not plump - face. Her bra straps, exposed on both shoulders, were red velvet. "Seriously? I can't believe it," she said.

"Hi, Cecilia," I said. "It's Cecilia, right?"

"You again," said Cecilia.

"Do you know this guy?" asked Sporty Spice.

"Sort of. He tried to serenade me on move-in day in front of everyone. You just don't know when to stop."

I hung my head.

"Nope," Eddie replied. "He's hopeless."

"What song did he sing?" asked Sporty Spice.

"Yes, pray tell, Cid," said Eddie. "What song did you sing?"

"'Cecilia' by Simon and Garfunkel."

Eddie and Sporty Spice cracked up.

"You know the song, right?" I said. *"Oh, Cecilia, you're breaking my heart. You're shaking my confidence, baby."*

"Stop," Sporty Spice begged. "I can't take it."

"Yes, please stop," said Eddie, standing up to introduce himself. "I must apologize for my roommate. I'm Eddie."

"I'm Alice," Sporty Spice said.

"And you're Cecilia, I presume?" asked Eddie.

"That's me," she said.

"And I'm Cid," I said, following Eddie's lead.

"It's too late to be all proper now," Cecilia said.

"And, no, my boyfriend doesn't go here," Alice added. "He goes to Virginia Tech. Count yourself lucky."

Cecilia said, "Now that you know, you're probably going to be all, 'I'm just interested in having a conversation and making friends.' Aren't you, Billy Idol?"

"I won't even try with you," I said. "I already learned my lesson."

"It was nice to meet you, Eddie," Cecilia said. "I'm sorry about your luck with the roommate lottery. I would check with the Housing Department to see about a switch if I was you." She pulled on Alice's arm as she moved to the door. "We better get going. Maybe we'll see you around."

"It was nice to meet you too," Alice said, stumbling backwards as Cecilia pulled her out of the room.

"Women," I said, shaking my head.

A moment later, I noticed Eddie was still looking toward the hallway instead of watching the movie.

"Got something on your mind?" I said.

"No. Nothing," Eddie said.

"What can I say? I'm a matchmaker."

"Yeah, okay."

"I'm just saying."

"What are you saying, Cid?"

"Nothing."

"That would be nice for a change."

"I'm just saying, I'll probably tell this story at your wedding. That's all."

"You're so overdramatic all the time," Eddie said.

"I'm a theatre major, Eddie. It's what we do."

"Are you sure you're not a girl, Cid? Isn't that it?" Eddie started putting on his shoes.

"If the shoe fits," I said.

"You're ridiculous."

"Okay. I'm sorry. I didn't mean to embarrass you. Where are you going?"

"To the library."

"Sure. 'To the library,' he says. You're going after Alice, aren't you?"

Eddie picked up his backpack and said, "Some people care about learning."

"Hey, man, get the degree, get the job. Grades don't matter in the real world."

"Some people want to succeed in life, Cid. Do you even know what that means?"

"I know you don't mean that," I called after him as he left the room. "You just have a weird sense of humor."

"See you later, Cid."

#

As it turned out, the key to understanding Eddie's behavior throughout his college years could trace roots back to that meet-cute. Eddie had blinders on. He was focused on two things: getting good grades and Alice, Sporty Spice.

I remember one day, during the winter semester, I ran into our dorm room and announced, between gasps for air, "We're going sledding down by the river. Get your snow pants on. Let's go."

Eddie was in his famous "studying spot" at the time. He was up on his bunk with his back against the wall and his feet hanging over the edge of the bed. He had books and papers spread out all around him and a laptop resting on his thighs, and he was typing with determination. Everyone on our floor knew, when Eddie was in that spot, he wasn't going anywhere until his homework was finished.

"No thanks. I can't," he said.

"Come on," I begged. "It's going to be insane. Plus, guess who's coming?"

Eddie stopped working and gave me his attention. "Who?"

"Alice. I know you want to hang out with her. Come on, man. Come on, come on, come on, come on!"

"First of all, she's got a boyfriend, so give it up. And, I can't right now. I'm sorry. Next time."

"First of all." I mimicked his tone. "Her boyfriend goes to Virginia Tech. That means he's probably a way bigger nerd than you are. And, second, he's out of the state, which means normal relationship rules don't apply. You know that."

"Thanks, but no thanks."

"Alright," I said. "If that doesn't entice you, maybe this will." I reached into my winter jacket and pulled out a fifth of Jim Beam.

"Cid," Eddie said, checking the doorway to make sure nobody was around. "You could get kicked out of school for that."

"Come on, Eddie. It's only alcohol. I'm not the one bringing the weed."

"What?"

"Yeah, but you didn't hear that from me. And I hear Alice likes to have herself some Jim Beam, too," I winked.

"You don't know anything about Alice," Eddie said.

"Maybe she'll have enough to want some of your Slim Jim, if you know what I mean." I slapped Eddie's dangling foot.

"I'm going to pretend you're not making jokes about rape," Eddie replied.

"Alright, Eddie," I said, getting serious. "What's your deal, man? Are you telling me a 'C' ain't gonna cut it? Is that what you're telling me?"

Eddie resumed typing.

"You're such a perfectionist."

Eddie kept working for a moment, then he stopped, thinking. He said, "The thing is, there are millions of people just like me - privileged kids growing up in a 'first world' nation in warm houses with electricity and televisions, all going to college. It's going to be hard to stand out, so I have to do more. I can't rely on skating by, getting mediocre grades and a run-of-the-mill degree. I have to keep my head down and work as hard as I can. That's what I can control. As an aspiring actor, you should understand that."

I nodded. Eddie got deep sometimes, too deep for me. He returned to his schoolwork. Jim Beam and I headed for the sledding hill.

#

Although Eddie was an attractive guy, he was awkward around girls. He may have come across as uptight or snobby sometimes, but I think it was more that most girls weren't Alice. One time, I talked him into going on a double date with me and Cecilia and one of Cecilia's friends, Lucy. Lucy was the kind of girl who needed to have a boyfriend, and not having had a boyfriend for a long time, she was getting desperate. Lucy was a girl of average height and size with strawberry-blonde hair and freckles that decorated every visible inch of her pink skin. Other than her high-pitched, nasally voice, I couldn't see any reason why she wouldn't be a good date for Eddie.

I proceeded to persuade Eddie - gently and civilly - into going on the date with us. For a week, I followed him around yelling, "Come on, come on, come on, come on!" But that wasn't enough to move him. I began to hinder him from doing anything he wanted to do. He turned on the television. I turned it off. He turned on the radio. I sang along as loud as I could. At last, he snapped when he was trying to make a sandwich one day, and I kept putting away the items he had just gotten out.

"Alright, I'll do it," Eddie growled, poking a mayonnaise-laced butter knife into my chest. "But you're planning it. I'm just coming along."

"Done," I said.

The following Friday night, when the four of us were out to dinner, we discovered why Lucy was single. Everyone placed their drink orders. When the waiter got to Lucy, she asked, "Where does your coffee come from?"

"I'm not sure," the waiter replied.

"Is it organic?"

"I think so."

"You think so? Is it fair trade certified at least?"

"Fair trade certified?" asked the waiter.

"You know, from coffee growers who pay their workers a fair price."

"I don't know. Our coffee is coffee."

"Alright," she said. "Just bring me mineral water on ice with lemon."

The waiter brought our drinks and we ordered our food. Lucy made so many modifications to her order, I'm pretty sure the dish she wanted doesn't have a name. Then she jumped right into conversation, saying, "Eddie, do you pay much attention to current events?"

Eddie said, "I had a current events class last semester."

"I think it's really important to keep up with what's going on in the world," Lucy continued. "Who do you like better, Bush or Kerry?"

"I haven't decided yet."

"The election is only a few weeks away." Lucy was appalled. "You are going to vote, aren't you?"

"Of course I am," said Eddie. "I just want to make sure I think everything over before I commit to someone. I think it's a big decision to make."

"You're right. It's a big decision. You know, I think political affiliation says a lot about a man." Lucy winked at Eddie and stroked her hair. Lucy talked so much and asked so many questions Eddie didn't have much of a chance to be awkward, but conversing with her was like trying to tack into gale-force winds.

Cecilia suggested that we catch a movie after dinner and retrieved a pre-prepared list of movie times out of her purse. "I wanted to see *Aliens vs. Predator*." Cecilia announced the movie title in a booming, low-pitched voice for dramatic effect. "It's showing at Rivertown at seven o'clock."

"I don't like scary movies," Lucy said. "You know that."

"It's not exactly scary," said Cecilia. "What about-"

Lucy interrupted her. "How about *National Treasure*? I'm not sure what it's about, but Nicolas Cage is in it. He's dreamy."

Nobody cared to disagree with Lucy. Doing so would only lead to some lengthy discussion of something worthless. *National Treasure* turned out to be a disaster.

"What's happening?" Lucy asked Eddie for the millionth time.

Eddie shrugged.

"Who's that guy?"

"..."

"Why did he do that?"

"..."

"Yeah, right, that's not realistic."

"..."

"I seriously doubt that would ever happen."

"..."

I was glad when it was over - the movie and the date. As I kissed Cecilia goodnight, I heard Lucy say to Eddie, "I had a great time tonight. We should do this again."

Eddie said, "Yeah. That might be nice."

"Good. Okay, goodnight," Lucy said, following Cecilia into their apartment building.

"Did you have a good time tonight?" I asked Eddie on our way home.

"Are you kidding me? She's crazy. She's literally crazy."

"Then why did you say you wanted to go out with her again?"

"What the hell was I supposed to say, Cid? 'I'm sorry. I had a horrible time, and I would prefer it if we never ever saw each other again. Okay, crazy-girl?'"

"I don't think you'd have to say all that."

"No," said Eddie. "I'm not planning to go out with her again. Did you actually think it went well?"

"No, but I didn't want to say anything in case you liked her."

"Don't worry about it. She's a nutcase."

"What can I say?" I said. "I'm a matchmaker."

"You're a real cupid."

"That's right, Cid the Cupid."

"Maybe you should date Lucy," Eddie said. "You're a nutcase too."

#

It was easy for Eddie to combine his two favorite hobbies - studying and studying Alice - because Alice shared the same drive and they often studied together at the library. The campus library had tables hidden amongst the book stacks, isolated to the point where they were difficult to find. Eddie and Alice spent every weeknight together at a table deep in the stacks on the third floor, way in the back corner - the furthest table from the entrance. Most of the students who went to the library never ventured all the way to the third floor and they certainly didn't make it deep enough into the stacks to take Eddie and Alice's table. When I went to the library, if I couldn't find an open table in the first few minutes my studying was doomed.

It sure was a bitch to get up there if I needed to talk to Eddie about something. That fool never carried a cell phone. He said he didn't want to be distracted from the people he was with by people he wasn't with. That was part of a larger problem we had during our junior year; we had communication gaps. Even when we all got together, Cecilia and I would have our inside jokes, and Eddie and Alice would have theirs. Half of the time we didn't know what they were talking about, nor they us.

One time, Eddie and Alice showed up to dinner trying to communicate with each other through a series of farts and taps - kind of like Morse code or something.

Eddie said, "Fart. Tap. Fart-Tap-Fart."

Alice said, "Fart. Tap. Tap-Fart-Tap."

And then Eddie got fake-offended and said, "How dare you call me an idiot?"

And she said, "What kind of person hates chocolate milk?"

This would get them into hysterics.

I said to Cecilia, "Do you want to ask or should I?"

"I will. What the hell are you guys doing?"

Alice replied, "It's from a book we've been reading when we procrastinate at the library. Vonnegut's *Breakfast of Champions*. Have you guys ever read it?"

We said no.

"In the book," Eddie explained, "there's an alien creature named Zog who comes to earth to warn earthlings."

"He could only communicate through farts and taps," Alice added. "We've been having fun with it."

"We see that," Cecilia said. "Fascinating."

Eddie said, "Cid, you should read his books. You'd like them."

"Yes," Alice said. "He's only the greatest living American writer."

I remember that conversation with the tapping and the farting so vividly now, because of what happened on April eleventh, 2007 - two and a half weeks before our graduation. That's when everything changed. For all of us.

That night I was hanging out at our apartment with Cecilia. We had just finished watching a movie and we had the local news on. There was a graphic on the screen of an old man who kind of looked like Mark Twain. The newscaster's voice was slow and deliberate. He said, "Unfortunately, we must end on a sad note tonight. *The New York Times* reported today that celebrated writer Kurt Vonnegut has passed away at the age of eighty-four. His works include *Cat's Cradle*, *Hocus Pocus*, and *Timequake* - among others. He is most well-known for his novel *Slaughterhouse-Five*, a harrowing account of surviving the firebombing of Dresden during World War Two. His death comes after suffering what doctors are calling, quote, 'irreparable brain injuries suffered in a fall at his home,' unquote."

Then an image of another man appeared on the screen. The caption read, in big letters: VONNEGUT DEAD AT EIGHT-FOUR, NOT TO BE FORGOTTEN. And, in smaller letters: Billy Phillip, Professor of Literature, NYU.

Professor Phillip said, "I knew Vonnegut personally. He was the epitome of human potential as a man and a novelist. He will never be forgotten."

Eddie came home not long after that.

"Did you hear about Vonnegut?" I asked.

Eddie just looked at me. There must have been a tone in my voice that said it all. He waited for me to say it.

"He died today."

I watched as the news registered on his face. He stood motionless for a long moment. Then he said, "So it goes."

I didn't understand.

He went into his room and shut the door. When I went to bed late that night, his light was still on, and I could hear Eddie typing in random spurts. He was instant-messaging someone - Alice I assumed.

The next morning, when I got up around eleven, I ran into Alice and Eddie in the hallway. They were both wearing black t-shirts with handwritten messages in Wite-Out on the front that read: SO IT GOES.

"What's that?" I asked.

Eddie slapped a book into my chest - a tattered copy of *Slaughterhouse-Five* - and said, "Will you get off your ass and read something?" And they left the apartment without saying more.

That was the first time in a long time that I saw Eddie and Alice together, but I didn't see either of them again for a couple days after that. Eddie didn't even come home at night. When he finally re-emerged, he was still wearing the same black t-shirt. He looked like hell, and he smelled like ass. I told him, "You're still wearing that t-shirt."

He shrugged and sat down on the couch next to me.

"You look like hell."

"..."

"And you smell like ass."

"What's the point?" he said.

"What are you talking about, man?"

"Vonnegut was right, man. This world is fucked. We spend our whole lives trying to rationalize a world that's unreasonable. What's the point?"

I didn't know what to say.

Eddie got up and walked down the hallway toward his room. He stopped. "I guess Vonnegut was lucky enough to be successful and recognized in his own time." He shrugged, then kicked at the carpet. "But now he's dead, and nobody cares. We're all just machines, going through the motions."

"So it goes," I said.

Eddie shook his head.

"I read the book, Eddie," I said. "I skipped class. Read it all day. I get it now."

"It doesn't even matter," he said. "What do we do with it? With life?"

"I don't know. Do your best, I guess."

"I guess that's it. When life gives you lemons..." Eddie walked into his room, leaving the saying hanging in the air, incomplete. Before he closed the door, he said, "Cid?"

"Yeah, man?"

"I love you. You know that, right?"

"Yeah, I know. Love you too, bro."

When Eddie shut the door, a thought flashed in my head. I saw myself discovering Eddie's dead body in his room the next morning. I tried to shake the image out of my mind. *Eddie wouldn't do that*, I thought. He didn't. But that's what happens in those weird moments, when somebody tells you how they really feel about you, you wonder if it was some kind of warning. And if you didn't act on it, you'd have to think about that moment for the rest of your life, wondering if you could've prevented a tragedy.

#

That was just the beginning of a terrible week. I didn't see Eddie again after that until April 16. It was a Tuesday, and it was cloudy and warm. I was halfway to my first class before I noticed the campus was deserted. I was dumbstruck, like a child who lost his parents in Wal-Mart. It wasn't a holiday. As far as I knew, classes were still on. I was confused.

I entered the academic building. The hallways were empty. It was so quiet I could hear my breath echoing off the walls. All my hair follicles stood en garde. All the lights were on in the hallways and the classrooms.

When I held my breath, I could hear strange, muffled noises down the hall. The sounds got louder as I approached the first classroom. I moved to the opposite wall to see in the door as I walked, but a janitor's cart was blocking the entrance. I stopped. Slowly creeping forward, the janitor came into view, leaning up against the cart. Behind him, from what I could tell, the room was packed with students and teachers. Standing room only. Everyone was silent. Faces were tense. I thought, *What the hell is going on? What am I missing?*

There was a television near the front of the room. I heard a broadcaster say something about death tolls and uncertainty. I leaned over the janitor's cart as far as I could so I could see. I caught a glimpse of the caption on the bottom of the screen, which read: DEADLY SHOOTING, VIRGINIA TECH.

I squeezed past the cart, praying I wouldn't make a sound, and took a place along the wall. Nobody acknowledged my existence; I was insignificant in comparison to the broadcasted images. There were no reporters on the screen, only images: policemen running, firemen running, students running, students huddling together, students crying, EMT crews running gurneys away from buildings. The images were a collage of chaos.

I stared in awe, like everyone else. I didn't dare speak.

After a moment, the images weren't even registering in my brain anymore. I was looking at the screen, but I wasn't seeing it. I snapped out of my trance at the sound of a lighter. A professor standing near the television lit a cigarette. "My God," he said.

Everyone seemed to nod in agreement. At that kind of moment, all bets were off. Nothing in the world seemed to make any sense anymore. Everything got put on hold and nothing was more important than consuming the images on the screen - not even a professor smoking in a classroom on a tobacco-free campus.

Then, I realized the connection: *Alice's boyfriend goes to Virginia Tech.* I left the room. The connection seemed significant enough to demand attention, but I couldn't think of where to go next.

I must find Eddie, I thought.

I ran to the library. The lobby, too, was deserted. I took the stairs. *They say not to use an elevator in emergencies,* I thought. I burst through the doors on the third floor. My senses were alert. Somehow I knew Eddie and Alice were there. I could sense their presence. As I ran through the book stacks, I could hear sounds of people moving with short, quick, hushed actions, making me run even faster.

That's when I saw Eddie scrambling to put his shirt on.

"Cid? What the hell?" Eddie stopped rushing and pulled his twisted t-shirt down to his waist.

I understood what was happening. I turned around and stepped behind a bookshelf, out of sight. I stood there shaking. My heart was pumping hard, too hard.

"What are you doing here?" Eddie asked.

"I'm sorry."

"What are you doing here?"

"Did you hear about what happened?"

"No. I was just - we were studying."

"I'm sorry," I said again.

I heard Alice moving behind Eddie.

"Hi, Cid," she said, indicating that it was clear for me to turn around. Alice was fully clothed. Her face was flushed red.

"I'm sorry to surprise you guys," I said, looking at the floor. I remember the pattern of the carpeting in the library - paisley - like it was plastered on the back of my eyelids. There were big swirls of red and beige.

"What's happening?" Eddie asked.

"There's been a shooting."

"Oh, God," Alice said.

"Here?" Eddie asked.

"No."

"What's happening?"

"There was a shooter," I said. "At Virginia Tech."

"Oh, my God." Alice froze for a brief moment, so brief it felt like years went by, a lifetime.

"I don't know any more," I said.

Then she ran past me, and she vanished, leaving behind everything.

I raised my eyes to see Eddie. "I'm sorry."

Eddie and I sat at the table in back corner on the third floor of the library for what felt like forever. When Eddie finally started to pack up his books, I gathered Alice's things. We said nothing. We didn't know who was shot. We didn't know if anyone was killed. We didn't know anything. But our lives had been turned upside down.

We walked down to the lobby in silence. We left the building and walked to the student center. There, we joined a crown gathered in front of a monitor. There was a reporter speaking, but I don't remember hearing a word she said. I only remember standing there, hearing silence.

When Eddie and I got back to our apartment, where we could act normal again, I asked him, "What happened at the library, man? Is there something I should know about?"

Eddie shrugged. "I think you know everything. I took a shot. It looked like it was going well, but then this happened. What do you want me to say? Everything's different now. It's probably over."

What could I have said to that? I knew he was right. I don't remember how we found out, but somehow we knew Alice's boyfriend wasn't on campus at the time of the shootings. It didn't matter. He was too close to the situation. Alice was planning to fly down to Virginia the next day, but her absence was already palpable.

Eddie continued, "It's too bad. In six months, barely anybody will be thinking about what happened there, except when another shooting happens."

Eddie was right. Even as I write this, nobody talks about what the media dubbed, "The Virginia Tech Massacre." All the talk is of the upcoming election right now and whether or not we're heading into another depression. As college students, at the time, it felt like those shootings were going to be our JFK, our Columbine, our nine-eleven. Sure, I remember exactly where I was when I heard about the twin towers - I was in Mr. Vasser's eleventh grade economics class - but when a catastrophic event is publicized every other year, there's too many to pay proper respect.

At first, even though the weather was beautiful, campus remained bare. Being on campus seemed unstable and insecure. Students and faculty hid from view. The feeling lasted for about a week; then some mysterious switch flipped. The innate response to flee from danger turned into a call to fight it. A rogue segment of every student-led group on campus emerged to protest something - anything really - and with violent rhetoric too. Then there was legitimate cause for concern. The Christian Students' Association was put in charge of planning a vigil to help students mourn for the victims of the shootings, and the event was shrouded in rumors of more possible shootings.

"I heard the Catholic and Jewish students are upset about being left out of the planning for the vigil, and I've seen several of them carrying guns."

"I heard there's angry pro-choicers with guns who are planning to attack the pro-lifers at the vigil-planning meeting."

"I heard the pro-lifers are planning to defend themselves with guns."

"I heard the Conservative Students for a Better America has organized a militia with guns to protect the campus during the vigil."

"I heard the Gay-Straight Alliance is planning to take out the Conservative Students for a Better America once and for all."

"I heard the president is going to call off the vigil."

"I heard the vigil planners are going to storm the president's office with guns if she doesn't approve of the vigil."

Everyone was afraid, but nobody was plotting. Thank God.

Channel Seven News

VANESSA VAN SLYKE (anchor): Welcome back, everybody, to Channel Seven News. Today, we're exploring the question the whole city is asking: Who is Edward Waters? Our correspondent, Allison Gordon, is on campus today, asking students about him. Allison, are you there?

ALLISON GORDON (correspondent): Yes. Hi, Vanessa. I'm here with two students who recall seeing Edward Waters on campus. First, Ben, you recall seeing Waters "partying," as you put it, several times. Is that correct?

BEN (student): Yes. Edward Waters was always hanging around with another kid. Some people made jokes about them being together all the time. I remember one time, when lots of students were sledding down by the river, I saw Waters and his friend with a couple of girls passing around a bottle of Jim Beam and smoking. I think they were smoking marijuana, but I'm not sure. I remember seeing him and that friend of his with Jim Beam though.

ALLISON GORDON: Thank you, Ben. And, Jessi, you remember Edward Waters acting strange after the Virginia Tech Massacre. Is that correct?

JESSI (student): Yes. I remember seeing him walking around with this black t-shirt on. Across the front it said: SO IT GOES. I remember that because I was offended. I couldn't believe there were people on this campus that seemed - well, not *supportive* of the Virginia Tech shootings - but, like, okay with it. Edward was one of those students. That bothered me about him.

ALLISON GORDON: There you have it, Vanessa. Students on campus recall Edward Waters acting suspiciously and partaking in subversive activities. This is Allison Gordon reporting for Channel Seven News. Back to you, Vanessa.

VANESSA VAN SLYKE: Thank you, Allison. Edward Waters had a reputation for partying and for being unsympathetic toward one of our nation's biggest tragedies. Stay tuned as we keep you up-to-date with this story. That's all for now. On behalf of the Channel Seven News team, I'm Vanessa Van Slyke. Good night.

Exhibit Two: Expectations

Our graduation ceremony was the same as the vigil; wild rumors circulated. When graduation day came, everyone was feeling tense. The administration had everyone patted down at the door before they could enter the arena and nobody protested the procedure. All the graduates were lined up backstage and nobody appeared to have a gun or uncontrollable animosity toward anyone else.

Cecilia, Eddie and I were waiting in line wearing our caps and gowns when someone behind us said, "Move it, jackoff. You're in my spot."

"What the hell, jackass?" I said, turning to see Alice smiling at us.

"Alice," Eddie said, giving her a big hug.

Alice was wearing silly regalia just like ours.

"What are you doing here?" I asked.

Cecilia hit me before Alice could answer. "Where the hell have you been?" Cecilia demanded, pulling Alice into an embrace. "My God, how are you? We've been so worried about you."

"I just got back from Virginia."

"I've been calling and emailing you like crazy. Would it have killed you to respond?"

"I'm sorry," Alice said. "The last few weeks have been a whirlwind. I had to finish my coursework while I was down there."

"Are you staying up here now?" Cecilia asked. "What's happening?"

"Let's talk about this later, okay?" she said. "Let's just enjoy this for now."

Eddie and I exchanged puzzled looks. But Alice was back, and for a brief moment, it was as if the Virginia Tech Massacre had never happened.

The four of us were herded out onto the basketball court with the rest of the graduates while our images were televised on a giant screen behind the stage. Parents and family members cheered as we were funneled to our seats.

First, the dean of something-or-other began the ceremony with a prayer. In a somber voice, he said, "Lord, thank you for our safety."

I've probably seen too many movies because, after a statement like that, I expected the whole arena to blow up.

"We pray for the friends and families of the victims and for the community in Blacksburg. We pray that they may be able to find comfort and peace, that they may be able to rebuild their community and their school to be the outstanding, reputable institution it once was, before this tragedy occurred. And we pray for our country, that we may be able to learn from this disaster, that we may be able to move forward into a better future. We pray that you would be with our graduates today as they prepare for the next step in their lives, that they may be able to go out into this world and be the best they can be. Help them understand that you have big plans for them and that you have prepared them to be successful as they go out into the world. In your name we pray..." The dean paused, and most of the people in the arena took his hint and joined him as he said, "Amen."

Eddie said it too.

Our class president spoke next. She was a medical student, one of Alice's friends. Some professor from the medical school introduced her, listing an absurd amount of achievements.

"Thank you, Professor Watson," she said.

"Elementary, my dear Watson," I said in a British accent. Cecilia slapped my knee. Eddie didn't laugh either. Everyone was being so serious.

The class president said: "I want to thank you - my fellow students, friends and family members - for coming out today to celebrate this joyous occasion. In light of recent events, considering all the rumors, I wasn't sure if this was going to happen. But I, for one, am glad it did. It's times like these that bring us closer to those we love - perhaps those we've even forgotten to appreciate. I can think of one example in particular. A friend of mine, who was in a relationship with her high-school sweetheart, was separated from her boyfriend because he went to Virginia Tech." The class president paused to let this detail register on the crowd. "A little over a year ago, their relationship struggled, and they broke up. When she heard about the shootings, she realized they were making a mistake. She boarded a plane without a second thought and flew down to Virginia. They are now happily engaged, and she is graduating with us, here, today." The crowd erupted with applause.

Cecilia made a scene. "Really? Oh my God, really?" Alice smiled and raised her left hand as a response. Cecilia hugged her hard enough to lift her out of her chair.

Eddie stared at the floor; it was difficult to watch.

Cecilia tried to contain her excitement as the class president continued her speech. "It's times like these that give us a purpose and a mission. As they say, 'To whom much is given, much is expected.' With our new education, it is our responsibility to go out into the world and improve it. I believe it should give us a sense of optimism, believe it or not. As we head out into the world, we can rest assured, we are now poised for success, and as we have been brutally reminded, the world is ready to be improved. So, fellow students, your mission is set before you, should you choose to accept it." The class president paused, intending that to be a joke.

I shook my head and said, "No one is in the mood for jokes."

She concluded, "Go and do good. Thank you and congratulations." The crowd clapped.

After that the president of the university talked in vague terms about "achieving the dream" and "competing in the global village" and "forging a new frontier." She finished her speech by saying, "Remember, you are the leaders of your future. Only you will determine the limits of what you can achieve."

The keynote speaker was even worse. He was some billionaire alumnus that graduated decades earlier. He started by telling us that his flight from Dubai had gone well, and he was glad to be at our boring, little ceremony - my words, not his - instead of having cocktails with the who's-who of some who-knows-what. He wanted us to know what a big deal he was and how appreciative we should be to hear from him. I tuned out for most of it, only tuning back in when he seemed to be wrapping things up. "If you take nothing away from this ceremony today," he said, "take me as an example. With your new degree, from this very institution, you can go anywhere and do anything. You are now officially part of the American dream."

The school officials led the way in clapping for this person, for whose mere presence we were supposed to be grateful. The keynote speaker, in lieu of this generous praise, felt he was being called back for an encore, for which he was not prepared, so he added, striking the air with his fist for emphasis, "Dream big or go home, class of 2007."

The crowd loved it. Shoot, I thought Eddie was going to cry.

Next, the chairman of the university board introduced a man named Simon Wellner, one of the only names I remember from that day. Wellner was being given an honorary Ph.D. for lifetime achievements in scientific research. I don't remember for what exactly, but I do remember when the chairman said, "And, as of last week, Simon Wellner is one hundred years old. Come on up here, Simon."

When the crowd saw Simon ascend the stairs to the stage, something crazy happened. Somewhere near the back, among the older folks, someone started a standing ovation. Eddie jumped up out of his seat and clapped. He, like the crowd, seemed to be invigorated by this man. Wellner survived to be 100 years old. It was like we needed to see someone in the flesh who had made it through. He represented something about the world that worked.

Finally, it was time to commence. When it was our turn, Eddie and I were ushered to the side of the stage where assistants collected our name cards, which had phonetic spellings of our names printed on the back so the speaker would sound like he knew everybody.

Eddie went first. A camera followed him across the stage so everyone could see his face up on the large screen. Eddie paused in front of the camera to ensure his family would see him standing there with his degree, in his cap and gown, with his honors cords draped around his neck.

I followed Eddie across the stage, and on the opposite side a photographer stopped us to take our photographs so that our family could purchase them after the ceremony. Eddie flattened his robe, adjusted his hat and smiled. He made sure to take a number from the photographer.

Right before the guy took my picture, I opened my folder to display the missing contents.

"Are you ever going to grow up?" Eddie punched my arm.

"I better," I said. "I'm a real adult now."

#

After the ceremony, Eddie and I waited for our families on the sidewalk outside the gym. Eddie was glib despite the news about Alice; he was ecstatic in a way I'd never seen him before. I, on the other hand, was a little nervous to meet Eddie's family for the first time, considering what I knew about Eddie's relationship with them.

"What does your family look like?" I asked. I was up on my toes, trying to get a look over the crowd.

"If you see a tall, skinny man with dark hair and two tall, skinny boys with dark hair, none of which look anything like me, and a short woman who looks just like me, then that's them," Eddie chuckled.

Just then I spotted a tall, dark-haired guy with a scraggily beard looking over the crowd in our direction. He turned to his side and said, "Dad, he's over here."

I thought, *There is no way this is Eddie's family*. But I was wrong. The three men greeted Eddie without hugs or affection of any kind. He introduced me to his father,

Walter, and his twin brothers, Matt and Dan. It was an awkward reunion, and I wondered how long it had been since Eddie had seen them.

A skinny, little women joined their group, who did, in fact, look just like Eddie. Eddie introduced her to me as Melissa. She had a dark, fake tan that made her skin look like abused suede. Her hair was done up, and she was wearing what I assumed she considered to be a fabulous dress. She kept checking herself out in various reflections to make sure everything looked just right.

Before I knew it, a larger woman with a thick Spanish-sounding accent appeared out of nowhere and yelled, "Congratulations, Eddie." The woman ran up to Eddie and gave him a heart-felt hug. I heard her whisper into Eddie's ear: "You did it. I'm so proud of you."

Eddie beamed with pride. "Thank you, Maria. I'm so glad you could come."

"I wouldn't miss it for the world," said Maria.

Walter said, "We should find a place to eat." That was the first thing I'd heard him say.

Eddie ignored the suggestion, introduced Maria to me as his former nanny, and then he said, "We have to wait for Cid's family to get here first."

"It's okay, Eddie," I said. "My family will probably take forever to get here. Why don't you take off? Traffic is going to be rough. My parents are probably arguing about something, and my sisters are probably lagging behind to avoid them."

"Are you sure?"

"Yeah, go ahead." I knew waiting around with his family was going to be uncomfortable for Eddie. He gave me a genuine hug - not the half handshake, half backslap kind of hug guys normally give each other - a real, affectionate hug.

"Go get 'em, okay," he said.

"I will," I said. "And, hey, remember, the world is your oyster now."

Eddie laughed. "Got the degree."

"Now, go get the job."

"Give me a call when you get a chance."

"I will, for sure. Take it easy."

And just like that, we parted. We were both avoiding the real issue. Cecilia and I were heading to L.A. to start our new life together as soon as we could get the car packed. Our plan was to elope in Las Vegas on the way. We didn't know when we'd be back to the Midwest, so Eddie and I weren't sure when we would meet again face-to-face, and neither of us wanted everyone to see us get emotional about it. But I really wish we had, because that was the last time I saw Eddie as I knew him in college, before he met Norma Baker.

#

The scene at the restaurant, so I've been told, was just like at the Waters' residence. Walter sat at the head of the table with Matt and Dan on the right and Melissa on the left. Eddie sat next to Melissa and Marie was at the foot of the table. The only thing that was different that day from Eddie's early years was that everyone was making an effort to be polite. This was the first time they'd all sat down together since Eddie's high school graduation.

Once everyone began to eat, Matt asked, "Eddie, what is your degree in again?"

Eddie thought, *Oh, here we go.* "Social work with a minor in English."

"What are you going to do with that?" Dan asked.

Everyone stopped eating and stared at Eddie in anticipation. The question that was on everyone's mind.

"I could do lots of things. I could work for non-profits, child services, counseling, stuff like that. With my minor, I could work in publishing, maybe, or journalism. I could go on to graduate school and become a professor, or I could go to law school. I'm not quite sure yet. I could even go into politics."

"Politics?" said Walter.

"Yes, politics."

Walter grunted.

"You're going to be a lawyer?" asked Dan.

"I don't know. Maybe."

"What are you going to do in the mean time?" Melissa was trying to diffuse the inquisition.

Eddie wanted to say, *I've got a job lined up in California. It pays well, and I'm really happy about it. I'm successful, and I did it on my own. I'm moving away from here, and you'll never have to see me again.* Instead he said, "I'm planning to move into an apartment here in Grand Rapids and get a job. I have some savings to cover me for now."

"From your loans," Walter said.

"Yes, partially. I thought I would work for a little while, then maybe I'll go back to school. We'll see."

"We'll see," Walter agreed.

After the meal, everyone was ready to complete the obligation of the day and move on. Walter paid the check. Eddie thanked him, and he nodded. The group left the table without ceremony.

In the parking lot, Walter made his last effort to do what he thought any father would do. He said, "Eddie, if you ever change your mind and want to go to back to dentistry school, we'll have a job waiting for you."

Dan added, "Yeah, I got some denture patients you can have."

Matt scoffed.

Eddie bit his lip.

Maria hadn't said a thing at dinner, but now she piped in. "Knock it off. Nobody wants to spend their life sticking their hands in everyone's mouths." Maria pulled Eddie aside. "You don't need them. You never have. You'll be fine."

"Thanks, Maria," Eddie said. He waved to his family, and they returned the gesture. "You'll keep in touch, won't you?"

"You can call me whenever you want, Eddie." Maria and Eddie embraced one last time before he got into his car and drove off.

Before him, now, was nothing but the real world.

GRlive.com
Op-ed: "Edward Waters' Girl Trouble"

by Leslie Frazier

Edward Waters is a sexual predator, and he should be locked up indefinitely - the sooner, the better. He has a long history of preying on girls that are either innocent, spoken for or off limits. And the evidence is only beginning to stack up.

First, there was the incident with Lucy - the young college student who had the unfortunate experience of meeting Waters on a blind date. According to Lucy, Waters never talked to her again "because she refused to 'put out.'" Honestly, what kind of pervert expects to have sexual relations on a blind date?

Second, Waters harassed another college student for years, all the while knowing that she was in a committed relationship with one of the victims of the Virginia Tech Massacre. Most people, by now, have either seen or heard the transcripts of the late night messages Waters was sending to her. He was pestering her to "study" with him late at night or meet him at the library for an "afternoon study session." It is clear to anyone who has studied these messages that Waters was cyber-bullying this woman in an effort to get her alone and vulnerable.

Finally, Waters pushed the envelope too far with Norma Baker. He somehow managed to convince Baker, who by all accounts was an upstanding inmate, to risk her life and to risk further punishment, all for Waters' sick sexual pleasure. Waters is clearly a con artist and a master manipulator. As long as he is allowed to roam free, no female will be safe.

Leslie Frazier is the President of the Grand Rapids Area Schools Parent's Association (GRASPA) and a mother of four daughters.

Exhibit Three: (Mis)Communication

Even though the fiasco at the restaurant deflated Eddie's excitement, driving away from his family and watching that part of his life disappear in his rearview mirror liberated him once more and he was able to regain the sense of empowerment he'd felt during the graduation ceremony earlier that day. For the most part, Eddie had been able to suppress his feelings for Alice and control his reaction to the news of her engagement, and for that he was proud. He was able to get a sense of closure, and graduating with honors and Dean's List credits to show for it, he was satisfied with his college experience. After all, a college degree was only one of the necessary steps to success in the real world and it, too, was now in his rearview along with Alice and his family.

Why should he feel anything but excitement? Why should he have to worry about what they were up to? They didn't care about him - not Walter nor Melissa, not Matt nor Dan, not even Alice. As far as Eddie was concerned he was on his way to a new life, to freedom. He was ready to move on and begin the next chapter in his life. Eddie had nothing tying him down. He had all of his possessions crammed into his little sedan. He was leaving college just as he had arrived - all in one carload.

On his way to move into his new apartment, Eddie felt independence coursing through his veins, and it was exhilarating. He even began to drive with freedom, weaving back and forth within his lane. As he did so he thought, *I can do whatever I want. Dream big or go home.*

Eddie was dreaming big; he had major plans for his future. His "practical" professional plan was to: get an entry-level job, work hard, help people, do good, advance and retire comfortably. His "pie-in-the-sky" professional plan was to: get an entry-level job, work hard, help people, do good, advance, write a novel based on his experience, publish the novel, begin a writing career, use advances and royalties and notoriety to help people and to do good, travel the country promoting his books and charitable organizations, and retire comfortably. His personal plan was to: get a job, date, get married, buy a house, buy two cars, have kids, work hard to support his family, send his kids to college and retire comfortably.

As Eddie drove home that day, he said aloud, "It all starts with finding my first job."

#

Eddie's apartment was in the West Village Apartment Community, which was located near the west edge of Grand Rapids. It was a huge complex - the biggest one in town, in fact. It had hundreds of apartments in dozens of buildings - all stacked together - five high and ten wide. There were dwellings of all kinds, where people of all kinds lived: young, old, rich, poor, single, married and civilly united. A college-aged kid with roommates lived next to a family of five. An old retired woman, who had been there for thirty years, lived next to a just-out-of-college kid, like Eddie, who was looking to begin his first career. Every age, race and social class in the city was represented within that apartment complex.

The people of that city-within-a-city, however diverse, managed to live in close proximity without any conflicts. The ability to obtain and maintain the peace rested entirely on one unspoken rule - never mentioned by anyone, but recognized and observed by all - which could best be described as: *you do your thing, and I'll do my thing.* The rule allowed people to go to and from their apartments freely, no questions asked, and allowed people to do whatever they wanted, whenever they wanted, as long as they kept it out of sight from everyone else. The unspoken rule also released everyone from even the slightest form of social consideration, like greeting a neighbor in the hallway or opening a door for someone else's guest. Nobody was expected to be friendly or neighborly. Nobody had to get to know anyone. Participating in the community was neither required nor considered. It was a free and peaceful environment.

Eddie parked his car in an open spot near the leasing office. It was late afternoon already and he was anxious to get moved in. He opened the glove compartment and rifled through an assortment of crumpled papers: vehicle registration, expired; proof of insurance, also expired; and archived receipts detailing services performed. When the compartment was all but emptied and papers littered the passenger seat, Eddie finally found what he was looking for - the receipt for the deposit he made on his apartment - which looked like this:

#

WEST VILLAGE APARTMENT COMMUNITY
NEW RESIDENT FORM

Apartment: Five 'A'

First Month Rent: $700 - paid April twenty-one, 2007

Last Month Rent: $700 - paid April twenty-one, 2007

Security Deposit: $350 - paid April twenty-one, 2007

Present this form on your scheduled move-in day to obtain your keys. New residents will not be allowed access to apartments without this form.

Congratulations, you're now a valued member of our community!

#

Eddie entered the leasing office with his New Resident Form in hand. He had rented before, in college, but somehow renting this apartment seemed more official. For some reason, he couldn't help but wonder if they'd made some kind of mistake letting a single guy, who didn't have a job, lease an apartment. They could rescind their decision at any moment.

Eddie stepped up to a faux-wood reception desk that was occupied by a bald, middle-aged man, whose nametag read: DOUG SHETLER, MANAGER.

"I'm Eddie Waters," Eddie said. "I'm moving in today."

"What apartment?" the man asked, not looking up from his computer.

"Five 'A.'"

"Do you have your New Resident Form?"

Eddie handed over the form. The man grunted as he struggled to get out of his faux-leather office chair, and he disappeared into a back room. Eddie watched with disgust as the chair re-inflated, returning to its original form.

The man returned with a pair of keys and said, "Here you go. Five 'A.'"

Eddie took the keys and waited.

Once the man settled back into his chair, he said, "You're all set."

"I'm all set?"

The man grunted.

Eddie expected something more to happen. He envisioned himself signing an endless stack of legal documents or something like that. The whole process seemed too anti-climactic. He didn't expect to have his luggage searched, like going through airport security, or to get asked a list of formal questions, like going through border customs, but the fact that there was no acknowledgement of his arrival at all was strange.

As long as they have their money, I guess, thought Eddie. *I'm just another number on the spreadsheet.*

As Eddie was leaving the office, the man said to his computer screen: "Congratulations, you're now a valued member of our community."

#

By the time Eddie made it up the four flights of stairs to his apartment, beads of sweat were racing down his forehead as he groped his pockets for the keys. His hands were swollen and clammy from the heat. He hurried to wedge the key into the lock. He forced it, and it jammed. The key wouldn't turn. He jerked it out, dropping it to the ground. He paused, closed his eyes, took a deep breath and then picked up the key. He tried it all again, focused and deliberate. As he opened the door, cold air rushed through the opening like flood waters breaking through a broken dam. The refreshing air cooled his hot skin and made the hair on his arm stand tall.

Home, sweet home, Eddie thought. He slipped into the apartment and locked the door behind him. There was a stiff, quiet emptiness inside. The air conditioner, which was mounted in the living room window, was already on and its constant buzz offered the only audible noise in the place. It was a one-bedroom unit, which consisted of one large living/dining room, a "cozy" kitchenette, a bedroom and a tight, little bathroom.

Living the dream, he thought, laughing to himself.

Even after Eddie got everything he owned into the apartment, the place still looked empty. He didn't have any furniture to unload because he didn't have any. Eddie and I always lived in apartments furnished by the college.

Although it was early in the evening, it was too late to do any furniture shopping. That night, Eddie set up camp in living room, spreading out his comforter on the floor and folding it over him to resemble a sleeping bag. He fell asleep watching old episodes of *Curb Your Enthusiasm* on his computer.

#

The next day, Eddie went to a furniture store near the mall called Wolfson's Furniture. It was a chain store that was famous for its Super Bowl commercials. The one that aired the previous year caused the company some trouble. The ad was animated and featured two wolves driving a delivery truck, wildly zooming through traffic. The truck ran over a squirrel and screeched to a halt in a driveway. The wolves were greeted by an angry, barking dog, and one wolf kicked the dog aside as the wolves hauled a couch into the house. The house shook as the wolves dropped the couch into place in the living room. A wolf-sounding voice-over said, "Wolfson's Furniture. We deliver. No excuses." Then, a squirrel-sounding voice-over said, "No animals were hurt during the production of this advertisement."

Eddie didn't see the commercial during the football game, but he saw it on the news for weeks after that. An animal rights group was suing the store. They claimed the advertisement made a mockery of "No Animals Were Hurt" statements, which protect the lives of hundreds of animals each year. Animal rights activists protested outside of Wolfson's Furniture stores throughout the country, and some protests turned violent. Dozens of people were injured. The issue dissolved when the Virginia Tech Massacre happened.

Eddie went to Wolfson's because of the scandal. He felt the commercial was harmless. He couldn't understand how activist could harm humanity in an effort to promote the humane treatment of animals.

Upon entering the store, Eddie was greeted by a sales woman with a face that looked plastic. Her skin was shiny and smooth, and it was molded into an expression that was a combination of surprise and glee.

"Hi, there," she shouted, weaving around furniture as she hurried in Eddie's direction. "I'm Sandy," she said. "Can I help you?"

Eddie pulled a crumpled piece of paper out of his pocket and unfolded it. "Yes, I believe so. I need a couch, a television stand and a bed."

"Okay," she said. "By bed, do you mean you need a frame, box springs, a mattress and a headboard?" The woman spoke in a constant state of excitement. It made her sound ironic and monotonous.

"No," said Eddie. "Just the box springs and mattress for today."

The woman scribbled some notes on a memo pad. "What about a headboard?"

"No."

"No headboard?"

"No, not today."

"What about dressers?"

"No, I don't think so."

"How about night stands?"

"No."

"Okay, you said you needed a couch, right?"

"Yes."

"So, you'll need a coffee table."

"No. I'm on a tight budget."

"Just the end tables, then?"

"No."

"Chairs?"

"No."

The woman stopped scribbling and looked at Eddie over the top of her glasses. "You already have these things?" she asked.

"No. Just the basics for today."

"Alright." She sighed in a way that seemed to say: *I'm not happy with you.*

It didn't take long for Eddie to pick out a couch and a bed. He made his decisions based on price first and on looks second. After each time Eddie finalized his decision, Sandy said, "Alright." And then she sighed. Eddie was beginning to feel like he was either making poor decisions or he was being a bad customer, maybe both. By the time he was done selecting the items on his list, he was feeling absent. He had been interrogated, and the fluorescent lighting was bearing down on him.

Sandy said, "Let's head over to the televisions and see what we can get to put on that stand."

Eddie nodded without listening. He would have agreed to anything just then, and he was looking at televisions before he knew it.

Couch, bed, television stand, television and next-day delivery: $2,400.

As Eddie left Wolfson's, he consoled himself, thinking: *I would need to buy a television eventually anyway.*

Channel Three News

TOM GANNON (anchor): The Waters story keeps getting more and more interesting as it unfolds. Channel Three News has been following the story all week, and we continue our coverage now. Our correspondent, Stacey Taylor, is out at the West Village Apartment Community. Stacey, what can you tell us?

STACEY TAYLOR (correspondent): Yes, Tom, I'm here at the West Village Apartment Community, where Edward Waters rented a small, one-bedroom apartment while he worked at the Fifth Street Community Hospital. I'm here with the manager, Doug Shetler. Doug, you checked Waters into his apartment. Is that correct?

DOUG SHETLER (apartment manager): I did. Yes.

STACEY TAYLOR: What was he like?

DOUG SHETLER: Well, he prepaid for his apartment. He turned in his New Resident Form, and I issued him his keys.

STACEY TAYLOR: Is that typical behavior for new residents?

DOUG SHETLER: I guess so, but he stood out to me, for some reason.

STACEY TAYLOR: How would you describe his attitude that day?

DOUG SHETLER: I guess I would say he seemed a bit arrogant.

STACEY TAYLOR: Arrogant? How so?

DOUG SHETLER: He spoke very quickly, in short sentences. He seemed impatient.

STACEY TAYLOR: Did he say anything unusual?

DOUG SHETLER: No. He said very little actually.

STACEY TAYLOR: Is that unusual?

DOUG SHETLER: Yes. That was unusual. He seemed skittish. I remember seeing his car packed with all his possessions. He didn't have a moving truck or anything; he had everything jammed into that little car of his.

STACEY TAYLOR: That's unusual?

DOUG SHETLER: Yes.

STACEY TAYLOR: What kind of resident was he?

DOUG SHETLER: He kept a very low profile around the complex.

STACEY TAYLOR: Were there ever any complaints about him?

DOUG SHETLER: No. I don't think so. Nobody ever saw him, really.

STACEY TAYLOR: There you have it, Tom. The more information that surfaces about Waters, the more unusual the case becomes. Doug, thank you for your time.

DOUG SHETLOR: Thank you.

STACEY TAYLOR: Stacey Taylor, Channel Three News, at the West Village Apartment Community. Back to you, Tom.

TOM GANNON: Very interesting. Thank you, Stacey. I'm joined in the studio, now, by Wolfson's Furniture sales associate, Sandy Matthews, from whom Edward Waters purchased a sparse set of furnishings for his apartment in the West Village. Sandy, thank you for joining me.

SANDY MATTHEWS (sales associate): I'm glad to be here.

TOM GANNON: Waters visited your store to buy some furniture?

SANDY MATTHEWS: Yes, he did.

TOM GANNON: What did he say he wanted?

SANDY MATTHEWS: He said he wanted a bed and couch, but he was adamant that he didn't need a headboard. He just wanted the mattress and box springs, which was very strange. He also purchased a television and a television stand, but those purchases seemed impulsive, like he wasn't sure how much he'd be using them.

TOM GANNON: How did he treat you while you were dealing with him?

SANDY MATTHEWS: He was crass with me. I would ask him questions to try to help him, and he would give me lots of one-word answers - just no, yes, or maybe.

TOM GANNON: He purchased a mattress, a couch, a television, and a television stand. How did he pay for that?

SANDY MATTHEWS: That was what surprised me the most. That's why I remembered him. He was just a young kid, and he came in and paid for that furniture up front, in cash. And he paid in large bills.

TOM GANNON: That is very surprising. Unfortunately, we're running out of time. A special thanks to our guest, Sandy Matthews of Wolfson's Furniture, and thank you for watching Channel Three News. Godspeed, Grand Rapids.

Exhibit Four: Opportunity

Most of the morning was already wasted. Eddie had stayed up too late the night before filling out online applications for jobs related to sociology and editing as well as administrative assistant jobs, as a back-up plan. After consuming a bagel with cream cheese, Eddie felt better. He sipped on his coffee as he got out his laptop and began browsing through the job listings on *GRlive.com*. He was ready to hit the job search again.

Most of those job postings had the same vague job requirements, such as: college degree required, excellent writing skills, proficient with computers and customer service experience preferred. And most of the postings ended with the phrase, "training available." Eddie thought, *Seems like anybody could do these jobs, especially after on-the-job training. I should be a shoo-in. I'll be employed by the end of the week.*

Eddie stood at the kitchen counter tweaking his resume for another online application while he waited for the deliverymen from Wolfson's Furniture to call. His phone rang. The noise echoed throughout his empty apartment. The screen read: UNAVAILABLE.

"Hello?" Eddie answered.

"Is this Edward Waters?" a man asked in a deep voice.

"This is," he replied.

The man said, "This is Somebody Somebody from Bethany Social Services."

Eddie did not catch the man's name because, instead of listening, he was thinking, *The deliverymen are here.* And the part about social services disoriented him.

"Are you there?" the man asked after a moment.

"Yes, I'm here. How are you?" Eddie said.

"I'm well, thanks. Did you apply for the Refugee Case Manager position?" The man sounded skeptical. He was either unsure about having the right person on the phone or unsure why he was calling Edward Waters in the first place.

Eddie was less confused now, but he was still stunned. He felt as if he'd arrived to class unaware that it was exam day. "Yes. I did."

The man continued, "I am calling to see if you would be interested in meeting with me to speak about the position."

"I am."

"Would you be available to come in this afternoon for an interview?"

Eddie was taken aback. This was all happening so fast. "I guess so."

"Good. Our office is located off of Alpine Avenue, across the street from Best Buy. How does three o'clock work for you?"

His hand wobbled as he held the phone to his ear. "That works," he managed to say. His voice was weak and trembling.

"Okay, Edward, I have you penciled in at three o'clock. I am excited to meet you and I will look forward to seeing you then," he said, without a trace of actual excitement.

"Thank you." Eddie hung up the phone and exhaled. When the tension subsided at last, excitement ensued. He pumped his fist, Tiger Woods-style. "This is it," he said aloud to an empty apartment. "I'm on my way."

Eddie closed out of the application he was working on - clicking "don't save" - opened the job posting for the Bethany Social Services job and began studying for his interview. What surprised him - other than the fact that the job description asked for just about everything shy of a hazing ritual or a gang-related tattoo - was the compensation: $45,000. It took Eddie a matter of seconds to spend his new salary. He saw himself living in a house on the east side of town, diving a new car and taking girls out on dates to fancy restaurants downtown on the weekends. He even considered going back to the Coffee Cup Café to look for new housing online, but when he started to pack up his computer to go his phone rang again. This time the screen displayed: WOLFSON'S FURNITURE.

After Eddie directed the deliverymen as they set up his new furniture just how he wanted it, he sat down on his new couch to prepare for his interview, but he was distracted by the idea of his new life with his new job. He soon found himself reviewing his current lease to see how much it would cost him to break it: two months' rent.

#

Outside of Bethany Social Services, Eddie stood next to his car and took deep breaths. He straightened his tie using his reflection on the hood of the shiny black BMW parked next to him.

You got this, he told himself. *Be confident, yet humble. You'll be driving a car like this in no time.*

Upon entering the office, Eddie was greeted by a woman sitting behind the desk adjacent to the door. "Hello, how can I help you?" she said.

"Hi," Eddie said, clearing his throat. "I'm Eddie Waters. I'm here to see - I have an appointment at three o'clock. I'm interviewing for the Refugee Case Manager position."

"Let's see," said the woman. She picked up a clipboard and ran her forefinger down it.

"Edward Waters. Yes. I see you." She made a note on the clipboard. "Mr. Miller is running a little bit behind. There are a couple applicants in front of you yet. If you don't mind having a seat, we'll get you in as soon as we can." The woman pointed to her right where four chairs were situated around a coffee table with several magazines spread out on top. Two of the chairs were already occupied: one by an old man wearing a corduroy sport coat with elbow patches and one by a baby-faced girl with curly hair, who didn't look a day over sixteen.

"Thanks," said Eddie, feeling deflated. He sat down in the most accessible seat and picked up a magazine from the coffee table, which turned out to be *Good Housekeeping*. Eddie pretended to be deeply interest in what that magazine had to offer.

Before Eddie could find an article to read, the old man next to him said, "Are you here for the Refugee Case Manager position?"

When Eddie looked up, the man's face was so close to his that it startled him. "I am," Eddie said, leaning away from the old man to escape his breath.

"Lloyd Green," said the man, offering Eddie his hand.

Eddie shook it, then made a show of looking at his magazine even closer.

"What do you do?" Lloyd asked. Before Eddie could attempt a response, the man continued, "I've been a teacher for the last thirty-two years, but my union is renegotiating, so I had to retire early to keep my benefits under the old plan. Now I don't have enough money to maintain, well, you know, the lifestyle I've been accustomed to - not until I'm eligible for my social security anyway."

"Hmm," Eddie said.

Lloyd stared at Eddie, non-verbally demanding a response.

"I'm currently unemployed, I guess," said Eddie. "I just graduated from college."

"Congratulations. I graduated in 1975, if you can believe it."

"Hmm."

"What was your degree in?"

"Social work. Minor in English."

"I see," Lloyd said. "Well, good luck to you."

"Thanks." *That's right,* Eddie thought. *I'm way more qualified for this job than you, Grandpa.* Eddie buried his head in the magazine and read some article about designs for folding napkins.

After a few minutes, the old man continued, "When I graduated from college, I knew exactly where I was going to work. I had several job offers lined up."

Eddie grunted.

"You need to network. Get your name out there."

"Hmm. Yeah."

"You need to follow up on your applications. That's the key. An old-fashioned thank you card never hurts. That's what we did in my day, and my generation knew how to get jobs."

"Kids these days," Eddie said, shaking his head, amused by his own sarcasm.

The curly haired girl laughed.

"What's your name, young lady?" Lloyd asked, addressing the young woman.

She scowled at Lloyd, then locked eyes with Eddie. They shared a moment of solidarity, silently uniting against this chatty old man.

"Sandra," she said.

"Nice to meet you, Sandra. Are you waiting for you mother?"

Eddie tried not to laugh when he saw the look on Sandra's face. She said, "I'm twenty-four years old."

Lloyd was befuddled. He began to stutter, making noises that sounded apologetic. "Are you here for the..."

"Yup. Same as you," Sandra said, looking back at the magazine she was browsing. That shut Lloyd up.

The three of them stared at their respective magazines until a voice from the back room called out: "Marjorie, I'm ready for Lloyd Green."

The secretary jumped out of her chair, stood at attention and announced: "Lloyd Green, Mr. Miller is ready to see you now."

"Thank God," Sandra said to her magazine.

Eddie laughed.

Lloyd Green pretended not to hear them. He stood up and straightened his jacket. Marjorie guided him into the back room and shut the door.

"Did you just graduate?" Sandra asked, without looking up.

"Yes," said Eddie.

"Congratulations."

"Thanks. How about you?"

"I graduated a year ago."

Eddie nodded.

"Yup," Sandra said. She was responding to a question Eddie didn't ask, but was in fact, wondering. "I'm still looking."

"Oh."

Sandra leaned forward and motioned for Eddie to lean toward her. She said, "These fucking jerk-offs got their heads so far up their asses they can't even see the sun."

Eddie's mouth fell open. He snapped it shut.

"I mean, who the hell is he?" she continued. "He was born during a post-war boom and graduated from college when degrees weren't a dime a dozen. Now, he's worried about keeping his fucking Beamer and his pension. He probably has a time-share in Maui. His generation ran this country into the ground and we're unemployed because of what? Because we grew up with computers and video games? Because we don't write fucking thank you cards? People just don't understand. It's not like we aren't trying. Jobs just aren't as available as they, supposedly, *used* to be. Too many people need work, too many people have college degrees and too many people have college degrees with years of experience. And these people are out there starting their second careers and complaining about their retirement packages. They're all applying for the same jobs we should be getting." Sandra sat back in her chair, folded her arms and scoffed.

Eddie sighed. For reasons he didn't understand, he felt compelled to maintain solidarity with her.

She added, "Employers give me one of two answers. Some say, 'Thank you for applying, but we have several applicants with your qualifications that have more experience.' And the others say, 'We don't feel this job is right for you. Our experience has been that people with your qualifications do not work here very long.' I mean, what the fuck? Not qualified enough or over-qualified. If I'm overqualified, give me the goddamn job, jackass."

"Yeah," Eddie said. "That doesn't help."

"Networking is crucial. That's true. You have to know someone. That's the only reason I have this interview. I shouldn't even be here. I'm not qualified for this job, but my parents go to Miller's church." She motioned to the back room. "How am I supposed to compete with Elbow Patches in there?"

Just then, the door to the back room opened. Eddie could hear Lloyd Green say, "Thank you, Mr. Miller. I'll look forward to hearing from you." Lloyd Green appeared, and a portly, rosy-faced man escorted him to the door.

"You're welcome, Lloyd," Mr. Miller said. "You'll be hearing from us sometime in the next week or so." They shook hands. Lloyd nodded to Eddie on his way out. Eddie was relieved to hear Lloyd fire up his BMW and drive away.

Mr. Miller came out into the lobby. "Sandra, how are you?" he said, giving her a hug.

"Hi, Jerry, I'm doing well," she said. "Thank you."

Jerry, Eddie thought. *His name is Jerry Miller.*

"Come on back," Jerry said. He turned to Eddie and said, "You must be Edward Waters."

"Yes." Eddie shook his hand.

"I'll be with you in just a moment. I apologize for the wait."

"It's no problem at all." Eddie tried to sound relaxed.

As they headed for the back room, Sandra said, "Good luck, Eddie Waters. I hope you get the job over Elbow Patches."

The waiting room was silent now, and Eddie was finally able to think again. *Sandra can't be right,* Eddie thought. *She probably can't get a job because of that dirty mouth. I'm qualified. I got the degree. Now, go get the job.* In his head, Eddie began to review answers to questions Jerry might ask, and he regained confidence with each one.

After a few minutes, the door to Jerry's office opened. Sandra waived to Eddie as she left and he waived in return.

That was fast, Eddie thought. *Alright, just be confident yet humble. Go get 'em.*

To Eddie's surprise, the interview went off without a hitch. There were no questions asked he was not prepared for, and they seemed to have a good rapport. They even discussed the Tigers' season at one point.

"Edward," Mr. Miller said, "we have a few more interviews to do, but you can look forward to hearing from us soon."

Eddie was thrilled. He left Bethany Social Services that day with hopes higher than the big white clouds up in the summertime sky.

#

A week later, Eddie received the following letter in the mail:

> Dear Edward Waters,
> Thank you for your interest in the Adoption Services Manager position at Bethany Social Services. After careful consideration of the applicant pool, another applicant has been selected for the position. However, your qualifications were impressive, and we will keep your application on file. Thank you for thinking of us!
> Sincerely,
> Human Resources
> Bethany Social Services

#

Eddie thought, *Adoption Services Manager? What the...*

After reading the letter several more times, Eddie decided to call Bethany Social Services and find out what was going on.

Marjorie answered the phone. "Bethany Social Services. This is Marjorie."

"Hi, my name is Eddie Waters. I'm calling to check back on my application for the Refugee Case Manager position."

"Okay," Marjorie said. "Hold, please."

Music filled Eddie's ear. A moment later, it stopped, and there was click.

A woman picked up the line and said, "Thank you for calling Bethany Social Services. Refugee Management. This is Sandra. How may I help you?"

Eddie hung up the phone.

#

It wasn't long after the Bethany Social Services incident that Eddie realized Sandra's vision of the job market was accurate and depressing. Several unproductive weeks of job-searching had come and gone since then. It was already mid-June, and the mid-summer heat and humidity only added to his increasing weariness.

Once again, Eddie was sitting in his car, getting baked by the sun in another parking lot of another business that was supposed to be hiring. He turned the air conditioning to high and felt the cool air breeze between his fingers. He was dreading another job application and considered going home.

Suck it up and fill out this last one, he scolded himself.

Eddie retrieved an old t-shirt from the back seat and began to wipe the sweat from his forehead. As he did so, two beads escaped and dropped down onto his tie. "Damn it," he cursed, taking the tie in one hand and rubbing it dry with the t-shirt in the other. He removed his tie, threw it over his shoulder to the back seat and sat stewing for several minutes.

It was late in the afternoon - the hottest part of the day. Eddie had been job-hunting since he left his apartment early that morning, just as he had done for countless weekdays. The job search routine had become mundane. Eddie was good at going through the motions of it, considering it had been his main occupation since graduating in the spring. He was good at the looking part, not the getting part.

At first, Eddie looked for jobs requiring bachelor's degrees, but as his funds began to disappear, his requirements lowered. His pessimism and despair reached an all-time high after he submitted applications to fast food cesspools, and high school dropouts acting as hiring managers rejected him. Both funds and morale were now running on empty.

'Not qualified enough or over-qualified.' Eddie kept hearing Sandra's voice in his head.

Every week Eddie searched the job listings on the Internet and in the newspaper, organized them by preference and applied for each of them all in order the following week. He averaged twenty applications per week, four per day. At the beginning of the summer he kept track of how many he'd applied for, but he lost interest somewhere in the seventies. He was at his last stop for the day and the last stop for the week, which meant he was preparing to apply for the job that he was least interested in getting out of all of the job opportunities for that week.

This particular posting was for a security guard position with a company called North American Security. The advertisement said, "Three full-time positions available." And, most importantly, "No experience necessary."

Eddie rested for a few more minutes, waiting for his pulse to slow and his body temperature to decline. He picked up a folder from the passenger seat. It contained a resume and a pad of paper for taking notes. He opened the folder and ripped out the top piece of paper on which, after his previous application, he had written, "This sucks ass."

He got out of the car, gathered himself, and proceeded toward the building. *At least try to act like you want this job*, he told himself.

The building was new. It had been constructed for the purpose of housing several small businesses but, as the sign on the front of the building indicated, there were several vacancies. *Maybe I should go into business for myself*, Eddie thought.

He checked his folder. "Suite Five, Office B," he said aloud.

Inside the building, the musty smell of cheap carpet and paint greeted him. There was a long, whitewashed corridor that led to a small clearing surrounded by four identical doors - one for each business and one labeled "Community Bathroom." Eddie approached the door decorated with a "NAS" logo. He knocked. The sound echoed throughout the empty space.

The silence was intense. The sound of his breathing, inhaling and exhaling, reflected off the wood panel door in front of him. He knocked again.

The silence began to make him nervous. At last he worked up the courage to test the doorknob. It was open. Light appeared in the crack. He eased the door open, waiting for someone or something to stop him, but nothing did. He couldn't see much, only a single chair against the opposite wall.

"Hello?" he called.

No one answered.

He called louder.

Again no one answered.

Eddie entered the suite and surveyed the room, which resembled a waiting room at any medical office. The single chair he saw was part of a row of four chairs lining the wall, but there was nothing else - no furniture, no magazines, no decorations on the walls. To the right of the door was a small counter. From what Eddie could see nobody was occupying the space behind it. As he moved closer he noticed a stack of blank applications on the desk. He paused to listen - still no sounds. The place seemed deserted, like one of those post-apocalyptic scenes in the movies where everything seems normal, except all the people are missing.

"Hello?" he asked for one last time.

No one answered.

Eddie leafed through the application to see how long it was. Feeling braver, he stuck his head over the counter. There was an old phone on the otherwise empty desktop. On the wall behind the desk was a poster which advertised "North American Security" in a plain text. To Eddie's left there was a doorway to a back room, but he couldn't quite see what was back there.

This is pretty insecure for a security company, Eddie thought. *I could steal everything in here.*

Eddie stepped back out into the hall, pulled the door shut and waited to hear the knob click. Noticing the bathroom again, he decided to make a pit stop before heading home.

The bathroom seemed to be unused. Eddie locked the door anyway. He took his time doing his business, enjoying the peace and quiet. When he returned to the hallway, Eddie sensed something had changed. He scanned the room with his eyes. One time. Two times. On the third time he found it. There was a crack of light coming from the door to NAS, the door he had latched shut. A faint sound reinforced his suspicions. Someone was there.

Eddie knocked as he opened the door. "Hello?"

"Just a minute." Someone was in the back room.

Although Eddie expected someone to be there this time, the confirmed presence of another person in the previously abandoned office surprised him anyway. "No problem," he shouted back.

A moment later a man appeared behind the counter. He was tall and skinny with gel-spiked hair, and he wore a dark blue polo shirt tucked into khaki pants.

It must be casual Friday, Eddie thought.

"Can I help you?" the man asked.

"I'm here to apply for the security guard position," Eddie said.

The man seemed surprised. "Why don't you fill out an application and we'll see what we can do for you?" The man pulled a clipboard out from behind the desk and loaded it with an application.

Eddie sat down in one of the empty chairs. Out of the corner of his eye he watched the man return to the back room, and was relieved to be alone again.

'You'll see what you can do?' he thought. *I've heard that line before.*

Eddie filled out the application as he'd done so many times before. He returned to the counter and dropped the clipboard loud enough to notify the man that he was done.

The man popped around the corner. "All done?"

Eddie nodded.

"Okay, let's have a look." The man reviewed the application.

Eddie fidgeted.

"Everything looks good," said the man.

"What?"

"I got a job downtown at the Fifth Street Community Hospital that just opened up. Easiest job we got. The fellow that had it before now just quit unexpectedly. It seems like it could be a good fit for you. It's second shift. For us, that means it's two o'clock to ten o'clock in the evenings. It's mostly riding a desk, a few nightly rounds. That kind of stuff. Regular schedule. Mondays through Fridays. What do you say?"

Eddie tried to say something, but the right words didn't quite form.

"Oh, yes," the man continued. "Pay. I bet you want to know about pay. It's ten dollars per hour. Nine dollars to start during training, which, for that position, I believe is only one day. I'd have to ask Stan or Brad; you'll be working for them on-site. Also, if you do the certification, you'll get eleven dollars per hour. That's the best we can do. We don't offer raises. Does that work for you?"

"Sure. I guess."

"Alright." The man offered his hand and Eddie shook it. "I'm Steve Johnson," he said. "I'm the dispatch manager. Like I said, Stan and Brad will be working with you on-site. You'll hardly ever see me once you get started. Can you come in tomorrow to get set up?"

"I think so," said Eddie. The whole process took him off guard; he barely knew what he was agreeing to anymore.

"Good. Bring a passport or two forms of identification for the paper work, and a blank check if you want direct deposit. We'll get you fitted for a uniform tomorrow, and get your fingerprints for the…Oh." Steve paused. "Are you okay with a background check? We can't hire folks with criminal records for security positions."

Eddie laughed. "Yes. That's fine."

"Good. We'll get that done. You wouldn't believe how many people don't show up when it comes time for that. Also, I'll send you over to meet Brad."

Eddie was astounded. It had been impossible for him to find a job and this one came without the simple formality of an interview.

"How about nine o'clock tomorrow morning?" asked Steve.

"Sure." Eddie felt like a weary hitchhiker consenting to a ride with a nefarious-looking man, knowing full-well there might be risks, but seeing as how there was nobody else for miles, there weren't any other options. "See you tomorrow," Eddie added.

"It was nice to meet you, Waters," Steve said with a big smile. "See you tomorrow."

#

Eddie parked his car in front of NAS and made his way into the building. Unlike the day before, the hallway of the business suite no longer appeared abandoned. It was less than twenty-four hours ago when Eddie snuck around the place like he'd broken in, but the hallway seemed familiar now.

Eddie entered the office and was shocked to find a young woman standing behind the counter.

She's hot, Eddie thought. He didn't think it, exactly, not in his usual thought-voice; the thought was there before he could think.

"Are you Edward Waters?" she said.

At that moment, Eddie didn't even know. His brain was bemused.

"Are you here for the Fifth Street job?" she asked, worried that Eddie might not be Eddie.

"Yes," he said.

"Edward, right?" she asked again.

"Yes. Eddie."

"Thank God," she said. She introduced herself as Ariel, then proceeded to shoot a flurry of words at him: "Steve said you would be coming in, so I thought it was you, but then you didn't seem to know what I was talking about, so I thought maybe you were just coming in for an application, and I was starting to feel like a fool. And just think, I almost gave your new job away to someone else today. Ha." Ariel slapped him on the chest.

Eddie flinched.

"Someone's a little bit jumpy this morning. It must be the new job, right?"

"I guess so," he said.

"Starting a new job is always stressful. I think that's why I've stayed here as long as I have, because I hate starting new jobs, but it's not so bad. They treat me pretty well. Alright, let's see. We have some forms for you to fill out."

Ariel smacked a clipboard down on the counter and Eddie jumped. A pen bounced off of the clipboard and fell to the floor.

"Sorry," Ariel said. "I've had too much coffee this morning." When she bent over to pick up the pen, Eddie couldn't help but notice the purple thong sticking out of the top of her pants. Ariel popped back up and Eddie looked to the clock on the wall as if he had been checking the time.

"Here's a pen," she said, clamping the pen back onto clipboard. "Fill these out. Are you available to get your fingerprints done this morning? I can call over to see if I can get you in."

"I think that'll work." Eddie felt like a new student at orientation. He was overwhelmed by unfamiliar stimuli. His brain felt like circuitry about to short.

"Great. Have a seat, and I'll call over there. Then we'll get you fitted for your uniforms and have you on your way."

"Thanks," said Eddie. He took a seat in the waiting area. When his mind cleared, he thought, *She's hot, but I hate it when people use coffee as an excuse for their erratic behavior.*

Eddie couldn't see her, but he could hear her. Ariel sat at the desk behind the counter. She was on the phone talking loudly. "Hi, Dale? This is Ariel over at NAS. Yes, North American Security. What? No. I just need to know if you can fit in a fingerprinting this morning. For whom? What does it matter? Do you have a spot available or not? I don't know. He probably could be over there by ten o'clock. What? Eleven? Okay. No, that's fine. He'll be there at eleven." She hung up the phone, stood up and leaned over the counter to see Eddie. "I hate dealing with those people. I can't get a straight answer out of them. Do you have a spot open or don't you? Don't you just hate people like that?" She was leaning way over the counter now, awaiting Eddie's reply.

"I guess," Eddie said, not looking up from his paperwork.

"I know. Sorry. I've had way too much caffeine today. Did you want a cup of coffee? I just made a fresh pot."

"No, thanks." *With the coffee excuses and all the talking,* Eddie thought, *I don't know if she'd be worth it.*

"What?" said Ariel. "Are you one of these nut-jobs that won't drink a cup of coffee? Are you afraid of staining your teeth or something? Afraid you'll get addicted?"

"No. I drink coffee."

"You just don't want a cup right now?"

"Yes. Is that okay?"

"That's fine. I can respect that," she said. "I can respect people who do what they want to do, but I hate these people who are all, 'You shouldn't do this. You can't do that. Don't drink this. Don't eat that.' You know what I mean?"

"Yes," Eddie said. He was relieved when Arial walked into the backroom. He scribbled as fast as he could to finish up the paperwork before she returned.

"What size are you?" she called from the backroom. "Are you large? What are you...three to four, or six inches?"

"Size?" Eddie was confused again.

"You know, what size do you wear? Are you a large in a shirt? Thirty-four or thirty-six inches in the waist?"

"Oh," said Eddie, wondering if his mind was playing tricks on him. "That is my size, actually."

"What is?"

"Large, for the shirt. Thirty-four, for the pants."

Ariel returned and flopped a shirt and a pair of pants onto the counter. "Once you're done, you can try these on." She sat down at the desk and began rocking back and forth in the chair, chomping on a piece of gum.

At least she's not talking anymore, Eddie thought. When he finished the paperwork he handed Ariel the clipboard.

"That wasn't so bad, was it?" she asked. "Let's see here...tax forms, direct deposit slip. I'll make a copy of your passport and we'll be all set. Now, go try these on." Ariel pushed the uniform across the counter and took Eddie's passport, then turned around and fussed with the copier.

Eddie looked around the small waiting room and began to feel uncomfortable.

...and he heard Ariel say, "Don't be shy, drop 'em."

"Drop 'em?" Eddie asked.

"Yes. Drop 'em." She winked.

Before Eddie realized what was happening, he was on the floor with Ariel. He pulled her NAS-embroidered polo shirt off and flung it over the counter. She was wearing a matching purple bra, and her breasts were in his face.

Eddie said, "You're wearing a purple bra."

"Don't you like it?" she asked and proceeded to kiss a trail down the side of his neck.

"It matches your thong," he said. "I saw it earlier when you bent over."

"You're a bad boy," she said. "I'm going to have to punish you."

...Eddie slapped himself in the face, trying to jolt himself back to reality. He was still standing at the counter wearing all his clothes, and Ariel was still fooling around with the copier.

There's a bathroom in the hallway, he thought, coming to his senses.

Ariel turned toward him with his passport in her hand. "Here you go," she said.

Eddie could see her gum moving across her tongue as she spoke; it was hot pink. He tried to act normal as he took his passport from her and shoved it into his pants.

As Eddie walked toward the door, she said, "Take your time, Cowboy."

Eddie stopped dead in his tracks and looked back at her.

Ariel winked at him. "You don't have to be anywhere until eleven, remember?"

In the bathroom, Eddie held the shirt out in front of him. "This will work." He did the same with the pants, then stuffed the clothes back into their plastic wrappers.

"Do they fit?" Ariel asked as Eddie re-entered the office.

"They'll do just fine."

"Alright, just wear them with black shoes and socks. Here's directions to the police station, which is right next to the hospital where you'll be working, so that works out nicely for you. Your appointment is at eleven. Ask for Dale, and good luck dealing with him. Take this paper with you and give it to him. Once he takes your prints go ahead and take a lunch break, but make sure you're at the hospital by one o'clock. Brad will be expecting you; he'll be showing you the ropes."

Eddie waited for her to breathe.

"Oh, I almost forgot," she said with a smile. "You'll need a badge." Ariel flung the top drawer of the file cabinet open and pulled out a silver badge. It looked like the kind of silver plastic toy guns are made from. Ariel handed it to Eddie. "You're a security guard now," she said. "Congratulations."

#

At the police station Eddie was directed to a small room, maybe eight feet by eight feet. The cinderblock walls were painted sky blue and the tile floor was a complementary shade of green. It looked like it could have been a poolside locker room in years past.

Folding chairs lined the front wall, one of which was already occupied by a woman. Eddie's brain provided him with a complimentary assessment of the woman: thirty-five, maybe forty; good physical shape; curvy, not fat; tan, not wrinkled; pretty face; attractive smile.

There was also a man sitting behind a foldable table in the center of the room; presumably Dale. He looked like Santa Claus - that is, if Santa Claus's hair was dark gray instead of white. Despite what Arial said, Eddie didn't think Dale seemed hate-worthy. *It's hard to hate someone who looks like Santa Claus*, Eddie thought. But Dale wasn't jolly, even though his rosy cheeks argued otherwise.

"Name?" Dale said.

"Eddie Waters."

"That your full name?"

"No. Edward Waters."

"Papers."

Eddie handed Dale the paper as Ariel had instructed him to do.

"Take a seat." Dale nodded toward the folding chairs along the wall.

Eddie sat down in the chair furthest from the one already occupied, leaving an open chair in between him and the women.

The woman smiled at him.

"What are you in for?" Eddie asked in an effort to make small talk.

"Theft." To Dale, she added, "What? Is talking consider 'not cooperating'? Go ahead. Have them put the cuffs back on me. What do I care?"

Dale rolled his eyes. "Only twenty-seven months left before I retire," he said, more to himself than in response to the woman.

Eddie thought, *Finding a wife might be harder than finding a job. I was just about to hit on a convict.*

"Waters," Dale announced.

Eddie looked at the woman, surprised both by the formality of the announcement and by being called first. The woman rolled her eyes.

Dale said to the woman, "You'll be processed when your rent-a-lawyer shows up."

Eddie stepped up to the table and Dale placed a pad of ink and an index card on the table in front of him.

"Roll each finger of your right hand in the ink, then roll each finger on the card in the corresponding square." Dale tapped the index card. "Firm. All the way. Got it? Start with the index finger."

Eddie did so.

"Firm," Dale criticized.

Eddie pressed his middle finger down on the card. "All the way."

Eddie hurried through the rest of his fingers.

Dale studied the results. "Okay," he said at last. "Good."

Santa says I made the good list!

Channel Seven News

VANESSA VAN SLYKE (anchor): Welcome back, everyone. Tonight, I have Steve Johnson with me. He is the Dispatch Manager for North American Security. Steve, you hired Waters at North American Security.

STEVE JOHNSON (dispatch manager, NAS): That's correct.

VANESSA VAN SLYKE: Can you tell us how the hiring process went?

STEVE JOHNSON: Of course. We followed standard hiring procedures. Waters filled out an application, and he was interviewed.

VANESSA VAN SLYKE: Who interviewed him? Was that you?

STEVE JOHNSON: Yes, I interviewed him.

VANESSA VAN SLYKE: What was the interview like?

STEVE JOHNSON: I told him about the opening we had, and he expressed interest. He was an impressive young man.

VANESSA VAN SLYKE: Did Waters state a specific reason why he wanted the job?

STEVE JOHNSON: He said he needed the money. Plain and simple.

VANESSA VAN SLYKE: Did Waters have to complete any sort of certification in order to be a security guard?

STEVE JOHNSON: We do a thorough background check, which Waters cleared easily, and we do in-house training on site.

VANESSA VAN SLYKE: I don't mean to grill you, Steve, but what I'm wondering is: how did Waters manage to get this security position, when he was so obviously felonious?

STEVE JOHNSON: We do our background checks through the Police Department, and Waters didn't have a record. He was squeaky clean; there was nothing on our end that suggested anything out of the ordinary. But he did have a college degree, which could have been a red flag. It was a bit weird that a good college student would want one of our security positions.

VANESSA VAN SLYKE: Thank you, Steve. Now, we're going to go out to the police station where Channel Seven News correspondent, Allison Gordon, is on site with Dale White, who is in charge of fingerprinting and background checks for the Grand Rapids Police Department. Allison, are you there?

ALLISON GORDON: Yes, Vanessa. I'm here with Dale White. As you mentioned, he conducts the background checks for the police department, and he administered Waters' background check. Dale, how did Waters behave when he came to your office?

DALE WHITE (Police Department staff): He seemed tentative mostly, although I remember him flirting with a woman - one of our regular offenders - who was here while he waited.

ALLISON GORDON: Do you remember anything about the woman?

DALE WHITE: Yes, she was brought in for theft. It was her third strike. She's now a convict.

ALLISON GORDON: So, you might say there could be evidence that Waters had a thing for convicts.

DALE WHITE: Yes. I think you could say so.

ALLISON GORDON: And what happened with the fingerprints?

DALE WHITE: When I administered the fingerprints, it seemed like he was resistant to giving us good prints. I had to ask him several times to press firm. You have to press firm to get good prints.

ALLISON GORDON: But the check came back negative?

DALE WHITE: He didn't have a record of any kind, if that's what you mean.

ALLISON GORDON: Thank you, Dale. This is Allison Gordon, Channel Seven News. Vanessa?

VANESSA VAN SLYKE: That was Allison Gordon reporting on location at the Grand Rapids Police Department. There are still a lot of questions surrounding this case, but one thing is clear: Edward Waters paid very close attention to the details. It makes you wonder if anyone else may have been involved, and I think this story, at the very least, raises some serious questions about the requirements for hiring staff in security positions.

That's all for us at Channel Seven News. Thank you for watching. I'm Vanessa Van Slyke. Good night, Grand Rapids.

That's all for us at Channel Seven News. Thank you for watching. I'm Vanessa Van Slyke. Good night, Grand Rapids.

Exhibit Five: Isolation

The Fifth Street Community Hospital isn't really a hospital. It is, but it isn't. The real hospital is located across the street. The Fifth Street Community Hospital is actually a nursing home - a boarding house for the elderly and the disabled. The people who live there need some kind of long-term care. Some residents are young, but many are old. Some are mobile and physically capable, but many are not. Some are quite healthy, others are chronically ill. Some are mentally aware, but others are lost. And some are happy, but many are not.

The aptly named nursing home is, in fact, located in downtown Grand Rapids on Fifth Street between Fourth Street and Sixth Street. The hospital shares a large parking lot with the Police Station and the Women's Correctional Facility, which are housed in a large, decrepit-looking building that looms over the surrounding area, casting an imposing shadow. Some people gawk at the building as they drive by. Perhaps they are hoping to catch a glimpse of a criminal or some sort of shakedown. Other people will drive out of their way to avoid the area entirely. Speeding is not an issue on Fifth Street.

Outside the hospital, four onlookers - two elderly women, an old man and a young fellow - sat in wheelchairs in a neat row, tires locked side-by-side, scrutinizing everything that moved in front of the building's entrance. They watched as an ambulance entered the far end of the lot near the police station, turned left, followed a lane alongside the endless rows of cars and pulled up to the nursing home's front door.

The ambulance's engine roared in their ears and the heat of the exhaust covered them like a thick, wool blanket on that mid-summer day.

The driver jumped down from his seat, leaving the ambulance running and the driver-side door wide open, and proceeded to the rear of the vehicle. He grunted as he forced the clumsy, metal doors open. There, an elderly man waited to be released from the glass and metal cage.

"How was the ride, Sam?" the driver asked his passenger.

"Same," Sam replied, "as always." He spoke like he was in no hurry to finish his sentences, as if doing so would get him nowhere.

Bob - the old man amongst the onlookers - rolled his chair to the front of the sidewalk near the rear of the ambulance. His pale, freckled skin was furrowed at the center of his forehead, and his jaw was clenched. Those more familiar with Bob could easily identify his current expression as a warning of the imminent explosion.

"Can't you read the sign?" Bob yelled over the noise.

The driver, busy unloading his rider, appeared oblivious to the complaint.

Bob pointed in the direction of a nearby sign. "Please turn engines off while parked in the driveway!" The friendly manner suggested by "please" came only from the sign.

The driver pushed Sam up the sidewalk and deposited him in line with the other onlookers. The driver slammed the rear doors shut and returned to the driver seat. The ambulance jerked as it shifted into gear and sped away.

Sam felt the wind rush by him as it chased after the ambulance. With the power remaining in his right arm and his right leg, Sam inched his way down the sidewalk toward Bob. "Good morning, Bob."

"Kid's got no respect," Bob said. "Parents don't teach their kids anything nowadays. He sees the sign every day, but he's too lazy to turn off that got-dang engine."

"Oh, hush up," Bea, one of the elderly women sitting next to Sam, scolded. It was Saturday, which meant it was beauty-shop day for Bea. Her short, gray hair was carefully curled, which put her in a good mood. "Your belly-aching won't do anything but bring us all down," she said. "Not today, Bob. Not today." As Bea spoke she inspected her new hairdo by tapping her hands along the circumference of her hair, feeling the shape against her open palms.

"It's Saturday," Sam said. He gazed out over the hospital's courtyard.

Bob moved back into his reserved spot between Shirley and David and let out a deep sigh that signified surrender. He sat between Shirley and David because, if he didn't, everyone would have to listen to them argue all day long, and Bea and Sam didn't have the grit for the job.

David was a young man with a young mind, but his lack of motor skills rendered him nearly helpless. His speech was accurate but difficult. The best he could do was spurt out a few short words between intervals of deep breathes. A short conversation could drain the energy out of him. Shirley, on the other hand, was ninety years old. She was a skinny little lady from the South who sat outside smoking cigarettes all day, and her hands shook as she guided each one to her mouth. Her mind wasn't sharp anymore. She would often forget her place in a conversation and start over from the beginning, telling the same stories to the same people over and over. Between David's long-windedness and Shirley's forgetfulness, an argument would last long enough to leave David choking for air.

"Hello, Bob," Shirley said. "When did you get here?"

"I've been sitting next to you all morning," Bob snapped.

David erupted with laughter. "She...forgot...you were...here."

The courtyard, as it was called, was sad. There was one large tree that provided shade for the only patch of green grass on the grounds. In the center of the sole patch of green grass was a small, brick patio with a park bench. The patio was outlined by a flower box on three sides, but only a few, limp flowers were sprouting up through the bark-covered soil.

The front door to the hospital opened and caught the attention of all five residents. They watched anxiously to see who or what was exiting the building. A moment later a tall, young man with dark, crew-cut hair appeared in the doorway. He was wearing a security guard uniform - black shoes, dark gray pants with navy blue stripes down the sides, a navy blue shirt and a silver badge. A red patch on his shoulder displayed the letters "NAS," and a nametag pinned to the front of his shirt indicated that his name was Brad.

Brad's presence was nothing new or exciting to the audience, but the new security guard trailing behind him piqued their interests. Eddie followed Brad, wearing the same costume.

"Everyone, this is Eddie," Brad said. "He's going to be working the evening shift on the weekdays."

Eddie waved; he didn't have much experience with older folks. The patchy, gray hair and flaky, wrinkled skin made him a bit queasy. He couldn't stop staring at the maze of veins that decorated Shirley's hands, arms and legs.

"Hello," Bea said.

Eddie swallowed, trying to clear his throat.

"Bea's the leader of the pack," Brad said.

Bea checked her hair again.

Brad proceeded to introduce the gang, starting on one end and moving down the line. "This is David. He's not allowed to smoke. He might ask for a cigarette, but don't let anyone give it to him."

"I can... smoke," David said with a smile. He began to laugh, but he coughed instead.

Eddie tried not to look at the braces on David's legs, suddenly aware of all he had going for him, all the common luxuries of human life - the ability to walk, to talk with ease and to fend for himself.

"This is Bob," Brad continued.

Bob waved.

"And that's Shirley."

Shirley, with her weak hand, tried to guide a cigarette to her mouth, missed twice, then triumphed. She took a long drag, blew the smoke out of her nose and ashed her cigarette into a tall, plastic tube erected next to her chair. There was a logo on the side of the tube that read: SAFE-SMOKER. Eddie noticed Shirley was also wearing a Safe-Smoker bib.

"That's Sam on the end. That's everybody that's allowed to smoke. If any other residents come out to smoke, you'll have to tell our boss, Stan. The new administration doesn't allow the residents to smoke, but these folks were grandfathered - um - these folks were here from before. So, basically, your job is to keep an eye on them and make sure they don't burn themselves while they smoke. I know it seems like a silly job, but the state requires the hospital to have somebody out here. It's cheaper for them to hire us than to use one of their own employees, because we're not unionized." Brad leaned toward Eddie and whispered, "Technically, you don't have to watch David. He doesn't smoke. But it's good to keep an eye on him anyway."

Eddie nodded.

"Occasionally, you'll have others come down here too, but usually they'll be with family. If not, they might try to run away, so watch out for that. Monday, when you come in, I'll train you on the rest. By Tuesday, you'll be off and running without a hitch."

I can't believe this is my job, Eddie thought. *I'm a lame duck security guard.*

"It's a cakewalk," Brad added, as if he could see inside Eddie's head. "Somebody gets to do it. Might as well be us."

Cakewalk? Eddie imagined himself being called upon to run down a rogue resident. *I have no emergency training. I'm not sure I'm cut out for this.*

#

Back at the apartment, Eddie settled into his new couch, tired from his first day of training at the Fifth Street Community Hospital, although he shouldn't have been - all he did was stand around for three hours.

Eddie scanned through all the possible television stations that might broadcast an afternoon baseball game. Unfortunately, the Detroit Tigers' game wouldn't be on until seven o'clock. He hadn't been much of a baseball fan before last fall, when the Tigers made a miraculous run to the World Series. The Tigers swept the Oakland Athletics in four straight games in the

American League Championship Series, which was solidified by a walk-off homerun by Magglio Ordonez. It looked like the Tigers had momentum heading into the World Series. They had a strong chance to win it all, but with the help of several fielding errors made by Tigers' pitchers at crucial moments, the St. Louis Cardinals abruptly ended the Tigers' run in only five games. Watching those games with friends - with Alice - were some of his favorite memories. It had seemed like they were all part of the Tigers' playoff run, part of something larger than themselves, something great - if only for a fleeting moment.

This year, the Tigers picked up Gary Sheffield in the off-season to help with offense, so expectations were at an all-time high.

Being unemployed and without much to do, Eddie found himself watching the Tigers' games every day, and he was addicted. He even started checking the scores online and in the paper, and when the team had a day off he was left disappointed and bored.

No games were on any of the channels Eddie received, so he settled on watching a women's beach volleyball tournament on *ESPN*, telling himself that he was watching it because it was the closest thing to baseball on at the moment. He was not, of course, watching it to see the sweat-glistened, half-naked female bodies running around under the California sun.

One of the volleyball players caught Eddie's attention. She was blond, kind of short for her profession and hippy. Eddie imagined himself taking her home. He couldn't remember how he got from the door to the bed, but he was stark naked with the Volleyball Player's bare body bobbing up and down on top of him. His hands rested on her curvy hips. Her breasts bounced about her chest. And Eddie couldn't hear anything but the sound of the Volleyball Player thrusting her slippery sheath onto his sword. He hoped they'd managed to close the door and the blinds before they started. It was too late. The Volleyball Player yipped like a puppy each time her inner thighs landed onto his pelvis. Eddie saw himself growing inside her, tall and lush, like a tree. It was so intense that it was painful. Eddie's body shook from the pleasure as he erupted like a volcano, and it was the Volleyball Player who experienced the aftershock. Her whole body pressed down on him hard, and she screamed his name one last time before she collapsed onto his chest, deflated...

The volleyball tournament broadcast went to commercial, and Eddie sighed. He couldn't even recall the last girl with whom he went out on a date. He'd been preoccupied with Alice for too long. Then he remembered Lucy and regretted going down that road all together.

Eddie opened up a soda, took a long drink and began surfing through the channels again. His eyes stared at the passing images of Saturday afternoon television: soap operas, infomercials, twenty-four hour news channels and sitcom re-runs. He stopped on a wildlife channel where a male voice was narrating a lost baby elephant's search for its mother. Eddie watched the documentary until the baby elephant plopped down into a small pool of mud and appeared to be dying.

Eddie turned the television off.

Without moving from his seat on the floor, he pulled his computer out from under the couch and positioned it onto his lap. Online, Eddie's first instinct was to check his e-mail - no messages. He then checked the Tigers' schedule - no game tonight. Frustrated and bored, he checked the time - quarter to six. "Damn. What the hell am I going to do tonight?"

Eddie opened his instant messenger and clicked "available to chat." Several names appeared. Cid's username - C(men)Man69 - had a green dot in front of it, which meant he was also available to chat. Alice's username - AliKat - had a moon in front of it, which meant her messenger was on, but she was most like away from her computer. Eddie double-clicked on AliKat.

Eddie typed: Hey, Alice, how you doing?

You're an idiot, he thought, and he edited the line to: hi, alice, how are u?

Get off it, man, he told himself, trying to channel his inner Cid. *But Cid would tell me to call her. Tell me to hunt her down and make her mine.*

He closed the window and double-clicked on C(men)Man69. In the window, he typed: hey, man, u there?

He hit enter. I didn't respond.

Eddie typed: i got the degree, now i got a job i always wanted. i'm a security guard at a nursing home. can u believe it? LMFAO! it's not as magnificent as it sounds. i don't get a gun, but i do have a badge. livin' the dream, right? cya!

I didn't receive Eddie's message until nearly a day later, and I probably forgot to respond all together.

Eddie contemplated going over to campus and seeing what was going on at the student center, but he remembered the students who did that after graduating. Everybody knew who they were, and they were marked as losers. Eddie flipped through the contact list on his phone, considering trying to call someone. Most of his friends left for graduate schools, had jobs lined up in more successful areas of the country or went home to work for family businesses.

Then an odd thought occurred to him. Considering the ruthless job market, the ease at which he had been accepted at NAS struck him as odd for the first time. *How come they were so eager to get employees? Why weren't people interested in the work they were offering? Ariel was weird, but not that weird. What was missing?*

Eddie explored all the possible tragedies that could befall him working as a security guard for a nursing home, but no matter what possible problems he foresaw happening, none of them were worth giving up the job. Besides, what choice would he have? Funds were running too low to pass up any income.

#

Eddie wasn't hungry even though it was time for dinner, but with nothing else to do, he walked down the street to the Corner Bar and Grill. The sun had not yet retired over the horizon and the light was warm on his shoulders. By the time he strode into the parking lot at the bar, sweat had soaked through the collar of his shirt and left an oval-shaped spot on his back. Eddie sat down in the shade of a nearby tree to cool off; he was too embarrassed to go into the restaurant all sweaty, but soon thirst compelled him to venture inside anyway.

As Eddie entered the restaurant, he fell in line behind a family of four. The father held the door open for his wife, son and daughter. The pimple-faced boy laughed about something the father said.

"What's so funny?" the younger sister begged.

"Nothing, dear," said the father.

The young girl made her annoyance known by stomping after her mother.

The father held the door open for Eddie as well.

"Good Evening," greeted the hostess. "Five of you tonight?"

"Just us four," the father said, gesturing to everyone but Eddie.

"Oh, I'm sorry," the hostess said.

"I'm waiting for a friend," Eddie explained. "I'll wait at the bar, if that's okay."

"Yes, go right ahead. The rest of you can follow me."

Eddie put his head down and hurried to the bar.

The sun's glare penetrated the windows and danced off of the pop culture memorabilia that lined the walls. There were numerous pictures of celebrities ranging from Elvis and Marilyn Monroe to Kurt Cobain and Gwen Stefani. One wall exhibited the evolution of football equipment from the earliest jerseys, shoulder pads, cleats and leather helmets to the newest gear worn by the Grandville Bulldogs. The restaurant was bustling with the dinner crowd. The sounds of clanking dishes and mixed conversations filled the room. Faintly, a sportscaster's voice could be heard coming from the televisions hanging over the bar.

The bar was busy. The only barstool available was wedged between three, well-dressed businessmen and a middle-aged married couple. Eddie was relieved to get seated on it without disrupting either group.

When the bartender came over, he was feeling unnerved and over-compensated with confidence. "Beer, please."

"What kind?" asked the bartender.

"Oh, yes. What kind do you have?"

"We got all the usual stuff, buddy." The bartender chuckled.

"I'll have a Bud Light then."

"Okay. Bottle or tap?"

He didn't hear the question.

"Bottle or tap?" the bartender repeated.

"Oh." Eddie was getting rattled. "Tap."

The bartender stopped. "I'll need to see some identification."

Eddie's hands shook as he struggled to free his license from his wallet. He dropped it onto the counter and let the bartender pick it up.

The bartender inspected the card, then Eddie. "Okay," he said at last, dropping the card back onto the bar. "Do you want the sixteen ounce or the twenty-two ounce?"

"Sixteen." Eddie was glad to see the bartender leave, and he buried his face in the menu. However, as soon as he did so, the bartender returned with the beer.

"Are you ready to order?"

Eddie's hands began to shake again. He heard his voice quiver as he said, "I'll just have a cheeseburger and some fries."

The bartender took the menu and walked away.

What the hell is wrong with me? Eddie thought. *It's not like I've never eaten alone at a bar before.*

He sipped on his beer and surveyed the many television screens hanging about the room. The same *NASCAR* race was on most of them. Eddie pretended he was interested in the race as if that might be the reason he was there. He found racing to be contemptible when he considered how many gallons of gas were being wasted by the cars driving around in a circle, while he was forced to pay three to four dollars per gallon for gas that summer, because there was apparently a looming oil crisis.

How do we honestly let this go on? Eddie thought.

Eddie's gaze was so focused on the screen that he didn't see the waitress standing next to him. When she dropped the plate in front of him, he nearly jumped out of his chair.

"I didn't mean to scare you," the waitress said.

"You're okay. I was just watching the race." When the waitress walked away, Eddie looked around the bar to see if anyone had noticed. Nobody seemed to.

As the daylight dissolved, the light inside the restaurant changed to a soft, golden hue. With this change came a shift in patrons, as the families went home and the younger crowd came in. The businessmen and the married couple left and were replaced by a group of college students that had to split up in order to fit at the bar. They carried on their conversation over Eddie's head as if he wasn't there. Feeling the divide, Eddie ate his meal so fast he nearly choked, and he guzzled the rest of the beer to wash it down. "Can I get the check, please?" he hollered the next time the bartender passed.

It was not yet dark outside, for the Midwestern days are long in June. Eddie strolled down the sidewalk toward home without purpose, while the cool dusk air brushed against his face. The evening air felt refreshing. It had a distinct smell. It didn't smell good exactly - not like a scented candle - but familiar. It was making Eddie nostalgic, but he wasn't pining for any memory in particular, just something other, something in another time. Eddie felt at peace with the wind with neither push nor pull, simply co-existence.

Eddie returned to his apartment that Saturday night determined to get up early the next morning to go to church.

#

There was a sizable church located on the same street as the West Village Apartment Community, which Eddie drove past several times when he was finalizing the deal for his apartment. He whistled as he strolled along the street in his Sunday-best attire. It was a beautiful morning. The sun was low in the sky, shining a glaring yellow, and the air was moist and breezy, carrying around all the scents of the fresh-growing flowers, grass and trees. He, like the world, was rejuvenated and refreshed by a good night's rest.

Eddie was involved in the Christian Students' Association in college, but he didn't go to their services much. He wasn't religious exactly; he didn't grow up in a religious family either. His parents were holiday Christians. They went to church - Eddie and his brothers in tow - on all the major days: Easter, Thanksgiving and Christmas. Although Eddie was undecided about God, Jesus, sin, salvation and heaven, he believed in hell and he was determined to steer clear. He served on the leadership committee for the Local Mission Team, organizing local service opportunities for student volunteers, like collection drives and charity fun-runs.

Eddie tried to get me to go to the meetings, but I never did. Now, I wish I had. When he'd ask me, I would say, "Sorry, I can't. I've got homework."

He would reply, "You mean 'homework' like working on Cecilia at home?"

I would say, "Tell Alice I said, 'Hi.'"

"I don't do it to impress Alice."

"It doesn't hurt."

"Charity work today keeps the devil away."

"And ghosts and goblins and witches too?"

"Have you ever heard of a little thing known as 'a citizen's obligation to the community?'"

"More like an obligation to the resume."

"I bet it doesn't hurt."

It was a running joke we had.

The large church building was made with many different-colored gray bricks arranged in a symmetrical pattern that formed a decorative band around the outside walls. The building was surrounded by an even bigger parking lot that took him almost ten minutes to cross. When the church was in full view, the sight reminded him of a factory during a shift change. People and cars were flowing out of the church from the early service and were quickly being replaced by those preparing for the late morning service at eleven o'clock. Eddie was attending the late service.

Walking with his hands tucked into the front pockets of his neatly pressed black pants, Eddie mentally prepared himself for the attention an unexpected visitor would receive. On his way to the front door, he crossed paths with a perfect family of four. Eddie held the door open for the happy parents, and they exchanged smiles for "thank you" and "you're welcome."

As Eddie followed the family into the building, he found himself in a line waiting to shake hands with a smiley-faced, middle-aged couple that was standing just inside the door. Everyone greeted each other with big smiles and witty comments that were followed by friendly bursts of laughter. Eddie turned to abandon his horrible plan, but a line was already forming behind him. There was no way out. He was sucked into the vacuum, trapped.

As he got closer to the front of the line, he could read the print on the white nametags that were pinned to the greeters' shirts. One displayed the name "Lori" and the other "Bill." Both were subtitled: "Hospitality Team."

Hospitality Team? Eddie thought. *It's like their job to know everyone who walks through this door! Oh, God, here we go.*

When it was his turn, Eddie smiled and stuck out his hand. Lori grabbed it and shook it enthusiastically. "Hello, good morning! Welcome back," she said with a big smile. She released his hand as quickly as she had received it and reached for the next hand in line. Before Eddie realized his hand was free, Bill grabbed it and gave it a hardy shake. "Hello, good morning, sir," Bill said in a low, gruff voice. "Welcome."

And he was through. No scene. No questions. They hadn't even noticed him.

Eddie strolled away from the door and explored the magnificent lobby with the wide eyes of a toddler. The lobby teemed with people, resembling a mall more than a church. There were two floors with an escalator and an elevator transporting crowds of people between them. On the first floor, there was a full-sized coffee shop, just like a Starbucks, and next to that was a gift shop, which had a banner displayed above the door that announced a one-day-only sale on Bibles, book marks and key chains.

It was still early for the service to begin, so Eddie followed the flow of people going up the escalator to see what the sale had to offer. The escalator ushered patrons into the entrance of a large bookstore that was operating as if it was mid-week rush hour at the mall. Big blue signs were hanging all over the store, advertising the arrival of some book by a man named Tom Sullivan, who was evidently a popular writer.

Eddie walked to the center of the bookstore where there was a table piled high with blue books stacked in a neat pyramid. Several people were circling around the edge of the display, and Eddie joined them to inspect the new book. On the cover was a picture of an older man who had a full head of light brown hair and glasses and was smiling wide. The title on the book was *Seek and Find: God's Looking for You.* Eddie checked the price: $26.95. He instinctively returned the book to its place on the pyramid.

Eddie wandered out the door and took the escalator back down to the first floor, where he was herded into a large auditorium along with many other church-goers. He was astounded by the size of the place. There were three sections of stadium-style benches - each of which, he estimated, could hold at least five hundred people - all pointing toward a large stage, front and center.

Throughout the auditorium, at equal intervals, there were massive, plasma-screen televisions hanging from the ceiling and fixed to the walls. Each one was scrolling through the day's events and announcements while displaying a countdown to the service. Eddie was in awe at the amount of screens in front of him. He just bought a television that was smaller and of lower quality, and he knew that each one of those televisions cost small fortune.

In front of the stage, there were several people frantically scampering around like ants working around a new hole. They were all wearing identical black t-shirts with the word "staff" printed on the back, and all the crew members had a microphones dangling in front of their mouths, connected from the ear. They were running cables to and from three different cameras, one of which was mounted on the end of an electronic crane. It looked like a production crew getting ready to televise the Academy Awards.

The seats on the main floor were almost full, and he was glad, for he was more than happy to sit near the back. Eddie was ushered in by Paul from the "Ushering Team," according to his nametag, and Paul did not seem at all surprised that he was there.

Eddie took his seat quietly and watched the nearest television screen. He read the events and announcements, but he was really watching the countdown. When it hit zero, a huge curtain drew back and lights flared and music boomed from hidden speakers within the walls, and a huge choir dressed like angels in bright-white robes suddenly appeared on the stage, singing from the top of their lungs. The cameraman operating the crane swept the camera in front of the choir, and the image was displayed on all of the screens while the words to the song were at the bottom.

An explosion had taken place and Eddie was not prepared for it. Everyone around him was standing and singing the song. They all knew the words. He tried his best to blend in, mouthing along with the words on the screen. By the second chorus he'd gotten a feel for the melody, and he began to sing out loud. He was being swept away with the crowd.

When the song finished, they sang another song, and another and another. By the time the singing was finished everyone seemed content to sit down and be silent, and so was Eddie. As he settled into his seat, an unseen speaker's voice boomed through the speakers: "Ladies and gentlemen, please welcome your senior pastor, Tom Sullivan!"

The crowd cheered wildly as a curtain opposite from the choir drew back. The man from the cover of the blue book in the bookstore now entered the stage wearing the same smile that was in the picture. He waved to the crowd, mouthing, "Thank you. Thank you." Then, Tom Sullivan reached behind his back, and instantly his voice was heard. "Thank you," he repeated.

The crowd quieted down to a murmur.

"Welcome, one and all."

And the crowd roared with cheers once more.

"Wow, what an amazing crowd we have today. How wonderful!" Tom waited for the audience to quiet down, he took his place behind a glass podium on the stage. He began reading a passage from the Bible, which was also displayed on the television screens. Eddie followed along, watching the screen nearest to him.

Tom started to "break it down" for everyone, as he often said. Eddie struggled to stay interested in listening to the man who seemed to be full of anecdotes about "lost sheep" and funny little stories about people having "aha moments" that made them abandon their sinful ways and return to God. Eddie was relieved when the sermon was over, but then Tom prayed for a long time. He called out quick, short phrases followed by long pauses; the rhythm of it nearly put Eddie to sleep.

At last, Tom asked everyone to stand, which Eddie gladly did. Tom raised his hand over the crowd. "I want you to put your heads down," he said, lowering his head to demonstrate. "Put your heads down and close your eyes. Everyone close your eyes. I want everyone to feel comfortable and anonymous. And I want you to feel like you're alone."

Eddie put his head down and tried to pretend he was alone.

"Now that you are alone," Tom continued, "I'm going to ask you to respond to some personal questions. First, I want you to raise your hand if you feel like you've been away from God." He paused. The place was silent. "Now, I want you to raise your hand if you feel like God hasn't been showing himself to you, and you no longer know or have never known who God is."

Eddie felt compelled to raise his hand, but he resisted. *I haven't been near God. I don't know who God is.* He felt his palms moistened at his sides and his legs began to get jittery.

Tom continued, "And raise your hand if you desperately want to seek, and find, and get to know God better!"

Eddie couldn't resist any longer. It was all true; he couldn't lie. Not here. He raised his hand.

"If you're raising your hand," Tom said, changing his tone. "I want you to come on down here to the front."

Eddie dropped his hand, and he looked around. Everyone's eyes were open. Everyone saw him. He turned as gray as a cadaver, and he wished he was such.

"Don't be shy, now," Tom coaxed. "Come on down. I saw a few in the back."

Eddie froze in fear. He looked to the stage, panicking, but was somewhat relieved to see Tom pointing in a different direction. *Maybe nobody saw me,* he thought. He stared at the ground and tried to will himself invisible.

A skinny lady with a harsh-looking face grabbed his arm. She pulled on his shoulder. "Come on," she said. "You raised your hand."

"No." He jerked his arm free.

"Yes, you did. I saw you. Don't be shy."

"I am not going down there." Eddie glared at her.

The harsh-looking lady, suddenly startled, backed away.

Eddie stood at his pew feeling his heartbeat pounding in his head. He couldn't wait for the nightmare to end. He watched as a group of more willing participants gathered near the front.

Tom invited everyone to sit down, and he addressed the group. "All of you are here today because you are seeking God, and do you want to hear something exciting? God is seeking you!"

The crowd erupted with cheers.

"Today," Tom continued, "I am going to give you all a free copy of my new book."

The crowd went crazy with applause as an assistant came forward with a stack of the blue books.

"Read it. It will change your life," Tom said.

A final song began to play and the choir started singing again. Everyone stood and sang along as they watched the group in front of the stage make their way back to their seats. When the song was over, Tom dismissed the crowd.

Eddie hurried toward the door with his head down, determined to get out of there before anyone could look at him, much less talk to him. On his way, he nearly knocked over a woman who stepped into his path. It was the harsh-looking woman again.

"Excuse me," she said. "You should fill out a comment card so the pastor can contact you."

Eddie knew his face was burning with rage; he could feel it in his cheeks. "It was supposed to be anonymous."

"He can help you with your questions about God."

"It was supposed to be anonymous," he growled. He was exploding out of control, but he couldn't hold it back any longer. "He doesn't care about God. He just wants to sell books. He's a liar and a fraud!" Eddie pushed her aside and marched out the door.

Channel Three News

TOM GANNON (anchor): Today, we are honored to have a special guest. We are here for an exclusive interview with Edward Waters' former nanny, Maria. She's going to tell us a little bit about this mysterious Edward Waters and, perhaps, give us some insight into the case. Hi, Maria, how are you?

MARIA (Waters' nanny): I'm well. Thank you.

TOM GANNON: Thank you for joining us today, Maria. Can you tell us a little about what Edward was like as a child?

MARIA: Eddie was a delightful child. A curious little boy. Smart and creative. Loved to read books and draw pictures.

TOM GANNON: You were Edward's nanny for how long?

MARIA: Eighteen years, almost his whole life.

TOM GANNON: Edward's father is a dentist, and his mother is a homemaker. And he has two older brothers. Is that correct?

MARIA: Yes.

TOM GANNON: They seem like such a nice family, but there have been reports that Edward severed ties with them since moving out of the house. Can you tell us about the relationship he had with his family?

MARIA: Eddie was a good kid. Didn't fit in with his older brothers. His brothers are twins. They had each other. Eddie was often left to himself. I don't know what his relationship with his parents was like after he moved out, but before that, there was lots of pressure on Eddie to go to dental school. He wanted to go his own direction.

TOM GANNON: He certainly did. Maria, I have a picture here. It shows Edward on his graduation day. He's smiling and holding up what appears to be his diploma. He appears to be quite happy. What do you think of when you see this picture?

MARIA: I was there that day. Eddie was just so excited to get his degree. I hadn't seen him in years. Hadn't seen his childhood enthusiasm in even longer. That day, he was my little Eduardo again. Made me so proud.

TOM GANNON: When you last saw Edward, was there anything that stood out to you? Was there anything that seemed odd or out of place?

MARIA: Oh, no. He was just so happy to get that degree. To finally prove himself to his father.

TOM GANNON: Did he mention anything about a woman or plans to leave the area?

MARIA: No, he didn't. At that time, he was still unsure what he was going to do. We went out to dinner after the ceremony. Somebody asked him what his plans were. The question made him uncomfortable.

TOM GANNON: Uncomfortable? Like he was hiding something.

MARIA: No. Like he wished he'd had an answer.

TOM GANNON: Maria, thank you for your time. We will certainly keep a close watch on this case.

MARIA: Thank you, Tom.

Exhibit Six: Conception, Part I

Early on the following Monday morning, Eddie sat on his couch watching the sports highlights from Sunday's baseball games while he ate his breakfast - overly fried eggs on burnt toast. A highlight of Sunday's Tigers' game came on. The Tigers crushed the Cleveland Indians, nine to two. Gary Sheffield hit a two-run home run in the first inning to kick things off right, and the Tigers added runs throughout the game. Jeremy Bonderman produced a quality start, going six and two-thirds innings, giving up only two runs on four hits and striking out six batters.

Eddie took personal pride in the team's victory. After a lone Saturday, and the Sunday morning debacle at the church, he needed something good to happen and the Tigers delivered. The team was six games over five hundred almost one-third of the way through the season. Chances were good they were going to make the playoffs again, and that gave Eddie hope for the future.

Once the highlight was over there was a commercial break, and then the same episode of *SportsCenter* started all over again. Eddie, having nothing to do for the next six hours, stared blankly at the screen, but having nothing to do in the morning on a weekday was different from having nothing to do on a Friday or Saturday night. At night on the weekends, young people were expected to hang out with friends, or go out on the town, or do something else that is generally frowned upon by older generations. In stark contrast, such expectations were nonexistent on weekday mornings. Young people were expected to sleep in and do nothing productive, to the dismay of older generations. Eddie didn't find it difficult to lie on the couch for hours on end, knowing a full day of work began at two o'clock.

Eddie thought of the Volleyball Player again. He imagined her on top of him. Every time he fixated on something new, and this time was her skin. He felt the softness and smoothness of her skin with his fingertips. He noticed she had moles, beauty marks. She had one on the inside of her right hip just above her pubic hair. He moved his thumb over it. She had another one on her left breast, just below her nipple. He cupped her breast to rub it with his other thumb. She responded to his touch and moaned, and he erupted again...

#

The sun was shining over the Fifth Street Community Hospital as Eddie parked his car at the far end of the lot. He was too embarrassed to wear his security guard shirt on the drive into town, so he had to put it on in the car. He leaned the seat back and rolled from side to side, stuffing his shirt into his pants. As he struggled to shimmy his arms into the shirt, he hit his knee on the steering wheel. Doubled up in pain, he hit his head on the horn. "Son of a bitch," he cursed, rubbing his knee and his head. He looked about to see if anyone saw the atrocity - not as far as he could tell.

Eddie got out of the car to finish putting himself together.

On his way up to the hospital, Eddie stayed to the right side of the building and entered the front door on the opposite side of where the residents usually sat. He still wasn't quite comfortable with the residents. In the doorway, he could see the assembly had convened and the members had taken their spots under the awning.

The entire gang - Sam, Bea, Shirley, Bob and David, in order from right to left - was all looking in the same direction away from the building. Eddie followed their gaze with his eyes and discovered the object of their attention - a squirrel scampering up and down a nearby tree.

Eddie continued on and moved through the second electronic door that opened into the lobby. There, Brad was sitting at the security desk browsing through a blue three-ring binder that served as the "Security Log," as indicated by the words scribbled on the front.

"Hey, man," Brad greeted.

"Good morning." Eddie stood, waiting for more.

Brad looked up after a moment and chortled. "At ease, soldier," he said, nodding toward the open chair next to the security desk. Brad was recently released from the military and he still looked the part of a soldier. His uniform was clean and neat, and his dark hair was cropped close to the scalp.

Eddie did as he was told.

"So, you decided to come back, 'ey? Must not have been too rough on you on Saturday."

"No, not at all." Eddie couldn't help but feel like he was the subordinate of a dictating military commander.

"It won't be any walk in the park today."

"Really?"

"No." Brad laughed. "It'll be as easy as always, especially on the night shift. The residents head up for dinner around five o'clock and the administrative bigwigs all leave before six. You really only have to pretend you're working for about three more hours. There are only a few paperwork-type things I need to show you. One of them is to record what the residents do in this log." Brad's bushy eyebrows lowered to indicate the blue binder in his hands. "Whenever a resident leaves, write it down. Write down when they left, why they left, when they're expected to return and when they actually return. In case a resident comes up missing, they can look to see when the resident left and where they might be."

"Comes up missing?"

"Yes. In that case, they can also see whether or not you were doing your job, so try to keep up with this the best you can. If a resident comes up missing and it's not in here, it's your ass."

Brad dropped the security log onto the desk, then handed Eddie a clipboard with a piece of paper on it. "Also," he said, "this is a schedule of the evening rounds. It'll make more sense when we walk through it tonight. When you do the rounds, just leave the security log with Eva or whatever receptionist is at the front desk." Brad pointed to a woman that was sitting behind the desk near the main hallway. "She's Eva. She'll usually be the one here in the evenings with you. She's quiet and usually likes to be left alone, but she's friendly enough. She can help you with whatever you need. But, if you ever have any questions, you can always call me, too. My number is listed on the phone." Brad tapped the number on the phone twice.

"Sometimes you might have to help the staff with random things," Brad continued. "Sometimes we get these guys out here that just got released from the police station across the way. They come in here looking for some money or trouble or something. Sometimes they're pretty angry, and it can get ugly."

Eddie wanted to hear more details about the "random things" he might have to "help the staff with," but Brad mentioned it so nonchalantly, he didn't want to ask. Instead, he tried to play it cool, folding his arms across his chest and nodded as if to say, *That stuff would be no problem for me.*

Brad picked up the security log, got up and walked toward the electric doors. "For now we can go outside and hang out with the residents."

Eddie followed. Outside, Brad leaned up against the railing in front of the residents, and Eddie did the same at a safe distance.

"What did you do before this?" asked Brad.

"I was unemployed. I just graduated from college, but I couldn't get a job anywhere. Until now."

"You graduated from college?"

"Yes." Eddie avoided Brad's gaze. "Nobody's hiring, and if they are, they're usually looking for people more qualified than me. Otherwise, they were afraid I would leave just as soon as I could get a 'real' job."

"Would you?"

Eddie shrugged.

Brad nodded in agreement. This small exchange of solidarity helped Eddie relax.

"What did you major in?" Brad said.

"Social work."

"What do you want to do with that?"

Eddie sighed. "I could work just about anywhere. I also minored in English. I hope to write a book one day." After a moment's thought, he conceded, "But I guess the skills I learned are hard to transfer to the real world, not like going to school to be a dentist or something."

"I'm about to go back to school," Brad said. "I was in the Army for four years. I've been out for a while, working here. Now I'm enrolled at the community college. I'm going to be a cop, get a good job, and get the hell out of here, if you know what I mean."

"Yeah," Eddie said. *I know what that means,* he thought. *I hope that works out for you. It hasn't worked out that way for me.*

"This ain't a bad job if you just need to pay the bills for a while," Brad continued. "But I need to get a job that pays better, so I can buy my own house. Since I put in my time in the service, the government is going to pay for me to get my degree, and I can move on to a good job pretty quick."

The sun was beginning to heat up Eddie's shoulders, and he wondered how long he'd be able to stand it. He said, "I always thought that if I got a degree I'd be able to get a good job, and the subject wouldn't matter, but nowadays everybody is getting a degree. The degree isn't enough anymore. You have to know somebody - or know somebody who knows somebody - to get in almost anywhere." Eddie tried to resist ranting for fear of sounding like Sandra from the Bethany Social Services interview, but he couldn't stop himself once he started. "And even if you're the most qualified," he said, "the boss knows somebody whose kid just graduated and is looking for a job. Or you have to get a master's degree."

"That's tough," Brad said. "I got my connections in the police department here. They're going to get me in."

"That's good," Eddie said. *I hope that works out for you,* he thought. *Somehow, I know it will. It seems everyone's got connections but me.*

#

The afternoon crept on and the heat made the air stiff. Eddie began to sweat through his polyester uniform, which only added to the awkwardness he felt from being around the residents and Brad. Steady conversation died out long ago. He would eventually learn to enjoy the silences, but at that time the weight of the dead air bore down on him.

Bob broke the silence. "It's too hot," he grumbled as he wiped the perspiration from his bald head with one hand and fanned himself with the other. Bob's scalp and cheeks exhibited a red glow from too much sun the day before.

"If you don't like it, go inside," Bea said. Bea, who was sporting a thick wool sweater, couldn't have been any more pleased with the heat.

David burst into laughter, spilling a thick line of drool down his shirt. "If you...don't like it...go inside," he repeated in between slurps of saliva. Once David's laughter wound down, the residents returned to their states of hypnosis.

Brad leaned over to Eddie and whispered, "How old do you think David is?"

Eddie looked David over - from his thick, bound legs, to his round beer-belly, up to his scruffy face shaded by a colorful *NASCAR* hat. "I don't know," he said. "Maybe thirty or thirty-five."

"He's twenty-three," Brad said, pausing to watch Eddie's reaction. "He's been here for about two years already, ever since his accident. He was snowmobiling under the influence. His motor skills got all screwed up. He can't walk. He can't hardly talk, although he can think just fine."

"He's pretty much the same age as me."

"Me too. It's sad." Brad talked as if the residents weren't present. "Bea's a nice lady, easy to talk to, and normal. She can do most things; she just needs some help with her medications. I think she's here mostly for the company. Bob can get a little uneasy sometimes, a little cranky, but Bea usually keeps him in line. Sam and Bob are both here because they had strokes. You'll notice that they don't have much use of their left arms and legs. You might have to help them get around sometimes, but they usually do okay. Shirley, here, still forgets my name. The worst part is the stories - all the time with the stories. I usually pretend to be interested just to be nice. All in all, it's a good group. They won't give you much trouble. They just like to have someone to talk to, you know?"

Eddie nodded, looking over the crowd.

"I'll let you all get further acquainted," Brad said. To the group, he added, "You all be nice to Eddie. He's new." Brad walked into the building and left Eddie with nothing but his insecurities.

Eddie smiled and waved at the five sets of eyes that were now focused on him. He hoped they would say something, anything, to get the conversation started. They didn't.

"Hello," Eddie said.

"Hello again," Bea said. "You're back. What did he say your name was?"

"Eddie." He cleared his throat, trying to relax.

"Eddie," she repeated.

"Eddie," echoed Shirley and David in unison.

"Nice to see you again, Eddie," Sam said. Bob nodded in agreement.

"It's nice to see you again, too."

The gang seemed to be satisfied with the conversation and returned to their busy work of staring off into the distance at nothing in particular. Bob lit a cigarette, which set off a chain reaction. Soon, all of the residents were smoking, except for David.

"Can I...have a...cigarette?" David asked Eddie, grinning from ear to ear.

"No," Bob snapped. "You know you're not allowed to smoke. You ask every day. We're never going to give you one. Stop asking."

David laughed in short, sporadic bursts, sending saliva rockets into the atmosphere. He looked up to see if Eddie thought his joke was funny. Eddie looked away.

#

As the sun began its downward journey toward the horizon, Eddie began to loosen up. He found a spot out of the way where he could lean up against the building. The residents seemed to go about their business regardless. He watched as ambulances dropped off patients and picked up new ones, which happened almost non-stop.

Shirley asked, "Did I ever tell you about the time my daddy traded in the kitchen chairs to get us kids some school shoes?"

"No." *After all, it is my first day*, Eddie added in his head.

"It was spring," Shirley continued, "and we didn't have any money. It was a hard winter that year. Had to spend all our savings on coal. Us kids needed shoes, you see? You can't go to school without shoes. There were five of us girls, and shoes were expensive. But my daddy was set on us going to school. He'd say, 'There's two kinds of laborers in this world. Those that labor with their bodies, and those that labor with their minds. I'll be damned if any girl of mine is going to labor like I have to.'" Shirley puffed on her cigarette, and she seemed to forget all about her story as soon as she had thought of it.

In the silence, Eddie soon found his mind wandering into the archives of his memories. One particular memory stood out. It was the Sunday morning the day before He was going to start kindergarten. Walter was getting the boat ready to take Matt and Dan fishing out on the lake behind their house, which was customary. Their family had an aluminum rowboat that had lost its shine from constantly being left outside, and to get it ready Walter had to pull the lightweight boat out of the weeds, flip it over and push it into the water. Eddie remembered how Walter struggled with that boat, having to get it into the lake all by himself. When he finally got it into the water, he'd tie the boat up to the dock, stand up straight and try to catch his breath. By that point, he'd be panting heavily and sweating profusely. The thought of it made Eddie smile. After a moment's rest, Walter would begin loading the boat with three fishing poles, a dirty tackle box and a small cooler.

Walter helped Matt and Dan into the boat. Eddie remembered the look on his brother's faces, their eyes gleaming with excitement. Walter could barely contain his own excitement, but then he stood up straight and peered at Eddie, who was standing on the edge of the dock ready to get in the boat. "He's too young to go fishing," he said to Maria.

Eddie's little heart may as well have dropped out onto the dock, bounced into the water and sank to the bottom of the lake.

Maria started to protest.

"Maybe next year," Walter interrupted. "Not this year."

Eddie watched as the boat drifted away from the dock. Matt and Dan were sitting on either side of

Walter, rowing their respective oars. Eddie turned to Maria, pleading to her with his big, sad eyes.

"It's okay, Eddie. We can fish right here, from the dock." Maria took him back to the house to get a fishing pole. She left him standing in the yard while she went into the garage, and when she returned she was carrying an old fishing pole with a rusty metal handle and a grungy plastic bucket. "Here we go," she said with a smile. "We just need some worms."

Maria handed the fishing pole and bucket to Eddie, went to a large rock near the woods behind the house, and flipped it over. Eddie saw several long, slimy worms crawling around in the dark soil. "Here we go." Maria snatched the worms out of the dirt one by one with her bare hands and dropped them into the bucket. She filled the bucket with dirt and shut the lid tight. "Now, are you ready to go fishing?"

As they walked back down the path toward the lake, Eddie asked, "If I catch some fish and show Daddy I can do it, do you think he'll let me go with them next week?"

Maria hesitated. She said, "I don't know, Eddie. Fishing can be tricky. Let's catch one first."

Eddie couldn't help but smile all the way back to the dock.

Pole in hand, Eddie stood on the end of the dock and watched Maria rip a slimy worm in half and tangle it around the rusty hook on the end of the line. Then Maria stood behind Eddie and helped him cast his line out into the water. "Reel it in a little to set your line. When a fish bites, you'll be ready. Hold the pole in your left hand. Feel the line with your finger. If you feel a tug, pull back to snag your fish. Then, reel it..."

"I felt a tug," Eddie said. He jerked the pole, and the line tightened. He wound the handle as fast as he could.

"Whoa. Slow down. You don't want to lose it."

Eddie began spinning the reel much slower - not because Maria told him to, but because the weight of the fish was making his arm tired - but he pressed on. He cranked and cranked, and he watched the intersection of the line and the water. The tension increased for a brief moment just before the fish jumped out of the water and hung in the air from the end of his line.

It was only a small sunfish, but Eddie remembered how it gleamed in the sunlight. He watched as it spun on the end of the line, yellow sides flashing, while Maria tried to grab it with her hands. To Eddie it was the biggest, most glorious fish in the Universe.

Maria held the fish in one hand, ripped the hook out of its mouth with the other, and held it out to Eddie. He took the fish in both hands. The scales felt both slippery and rough. It was cold against his skin, but it was a magnificent feeling. The fish didn't move for a moment, so Eddie relaxed his grip, then the fish lurched wildly. He dropped it, fearing for his life, and the fish bounced off the end of the dock and plopped back into the water.

Little Eddie stood there, staring blankly at the rippling water.

"It's okay, Eddie," said Maria, trying not to laugh. "We'll keep the next one."

As Eddie recalled the memory, he realized that he felt the same way after losing that fish as when Alice ran out of the library and out of his life forever. It felt like his chest had collapsed.

While Eddie awaited his next fish, his mother, Melissa, emerged from the path wearing pink shorts covering the bottom half of a blue, one-piece bathing suit and large sunglasses that hid half of her face. She was carrying a women's fashion magazine and a lawn chair that folded out to form a headrest on one end and a footrest on the other. She planted the chair on the edge of the bank and pushed it down to make sure it was steady. Then she folded out the headrest, which made a ratcheting noise: *tick, tick, tick, tick, tick.* The noise gave Eddie and Maria a frightening start.

"Hi, guys," Melissa said, folding out the footrest: *tick, tick, tick, tick, tick.*

Maria waved. Eddie focused his attention on his line, fighting off all distractions, any one of which could cost him the next fish.

Melissa dropped her magazine on the chair and walked out onto the dock. "What's up?" she said, trying to sound natural, as if she'd done this before.

"Eddie's learning to fish," Maria replied.

"Mom, I caught a fish!" Eddie shouted. "I did. Maria saw it."

"That's true."

"But it got away." Eddie hung his head.

"That's very nice, dear." Melissa lingered for a moment, then returned to her chair and her magazine.

Eddie waited and waited. He brought in his line and cast it back out again, over and over, for nearly an hour. "Maria?" he said, at last.

"Yes, Eddie?"

"I think I'm done fishing."

Maria helped him reel in the line, clean the hook and set the hook safely on the pole. She took the fishing gear back to the garage. When she returned, she retired to a nearby picnic table to watch Eddie from a distance as he played along the bank, waiting for Walter to return to tell him about the fish he caught.

When Eddie heard faint voices coming over the water, he ran out onto the dock. He could see the boat coming across the lake. Walter was rowing the boat this time. As they came closer, Eddie could see Matt and Dan standing up, each holding up big fish, and the fish were much bigger than the one he had caught.

Eddie stood there, watching, hoping the scene would change before him. As the boat approach the dock, Matt yelled, "Hey Eddie, look at the bass we caught! They're huge! We each got one!"

Eddie was silent. He eyed Matt and Dan as they got out of the boat and ran past him to show Maria and Melissa the fish. When nobody was looking, Eddie slipped down the path and disappeared with Matt's words ringing in his head: *We each got one! We each got one!*

Eddie's memory was interrupted by a group of nurse aides exiting the building. One of them was laughing obnoxiously. The obnoxious aide approached Bob. "Are you ready to go up for dinner, Bobby?"

Eddie checked his watch. Sure enough, it was already five o'clock.

"I don't want any of your goddamn dinner," Bob said. "It's gross. I hate it. I never eat it. And my name isn't goddamn Bobby."

Eddie tried to stifle his laughter, but failed. The obnoxious aide glared at him.

"Alright, Bob," she said. "You know you have to come up and eat something because you have to take your meds."

Bob grumbled as the obnoxious aide wheeled him away. The other nurse aides followed her, each pushing one of the residents inside. They left Eddie standing there alone, and he took the moment to finish his thoughts.

Later that year, after the incident at the lake, Walter informed Maria over the breakfast table that he made Eddie a doctor's appointment. He said, "I want you to call the school and tell them Eddie will be late."

Maria was shocked. She usually took care of all the appointments with the boys. "What for? Is he sick?"

"No," Walter said. "It's just a check-up. Eddie, how would you like to get a ride with me this morning?"

Eddie smiled. He rarely had the chance to be alone with Walter, so he was ecstatic.

Walter parked the car outside a big, brick building with shiny windows that were reflecting the morning's sunlight. Eddie recognized the place. It was the medical complex where Walter's dentistry office was located.

Eddie followed Walter as they entered the building. The lobby was large and airy with a high ceiling, and it reeked of cleanliness. It reminded Eddie of how his Grandfather's funeral smelled, of bleach and flowers. Eddie's shoes squeaked on the polished tile floor and the sound echoed throughout the room. Eddie froze, petrified. He would rather be caught with his pants down in front of his kindergarten classmates than make a scene at Walter's office building.

Walter walked on unaware of the problem. He pressed the up button for the lobby elevator, and the doors opened immediately. Eddie couldn't risk getting in trouble for holding up the elevator either. He had no choice but to run after him, shoes squeaking all the way.

"Slow down, Eddie," Walter scolded.

In the elevator, Walter pressed the button for the third floor. When the doors opened, Walter guided

Eddie to a big white counter that was too tall for Eddie to see over. "I have an appointment for Edward Waters," Walter said to some unseen person.

The unidentified person replied, "Yes, Dr. Waters, come right on back. The doctor will be glad to see you and Edward now."

Walter led Eddie through a side door and met the owner of the voice on the other side - a young nurse with curly, brown hair. "Right this way Mr. Waters," she said to Eddie as she led him to an examination room. On one of the walls hung a cross-section rendering of a heart split in half from top to bottom.

"You can sit up here, Mr. Waters," the nurse said, patting the paper that covered the patient's table. She helped Eddie climb up onto it, and then she left the room and shut the door.

Eddie was scared. Walter seemed aloof. The pictures on the walls were gross, and the room made him claustrophobic.

Someone knocked on the door, and it open slowly. A short man with a round face wearing a white lab coat entered the room. "Hi, Walter," he said with a smile, extending his hand.

Walter grabbed his hand and shook it. "How are you doing, Todd?"

"Good. Good. Things are going well. Just business as usual, you know."

"Good," Walter said. "Actually, can I see you outside for just a moment?"

"Sure, sure," said the doctor. They exited the room for just a moment and then returned. The smile remained on the doctor's face. He said, "Eddie, we're just going to do a quick check-up and you'll be on your way." He took what looked like an extra-large Q-Tips swab from a container on the counter. "I'll have you open up your mouth, and I'm just going to wipe this along the inside of your cheeks. Okay?"

Eddie opened his mouth. The doctor pulled the swab out of his mouth and gently placed it back in the container from which it came and sealed it. He was relieved when the doctor did what he said he would do.

"That's it. You're done. That wasn't so bad, was it?"

About a week later, Eddie was playing in the basement, directly below Walter's office, as he often did, and he could hear Walter walking around upstairs. After school that day, Eddie heard two voices coming from the office upstairs. The first voice was Walter's. The second voice was familiar, but Eddie couldn't tell who it was right away. Eddie pretended he was a detective, like the ones on television, and he stood up on his bed and turned his ear to the vent. Then he recognized the voice. It was Dr. Todd. Eddie listened.

"I have the results," Dr. Todd said.

"You might as well just give it to me straight, Todd. Get it over with," said Walter.

"The test came back positive."

"Are you sure?"

"Yes, it was positive. He's yours."

"How certain are you?"

"I would be difficult to be more certain. He's almost certainly yours."

Walter was silent.

"That's good news, isn't it?"

"Yes. Yes. That's great," Walter said.

Eddie was troubled by the conversation. He wondered if there was something wrong with him. It was all very confusing. What Dr. Todd said to Walter didn't make any sense to him at the time.

He kicked at a crack in the sidewalk with one of his clumsy security boots, and an image of Shirley as a child came into his head. He saw her standing barefoot in the dirt, watching her mother cry as her father sold the kitchen chairs for petty cash. *What can I honestly complain about?*

One

"You're back," she said.

"I brought you some food," he said. "I didn't have money for much, just an apple, some crackers and a Payday bar."

"Thank you."

"You must be really hungry. I'll bring more tomorrow. What kind of food do you like?"

"Everything."

"You can have anything, just name it."

"I would be happy with anything."

"Anything you want."

"I don't want to be a burden." She blushed.

"You won't be a burden. What do you want?"

"How about caviar?"

He laughed. "Okay. Anything within reason."

"How about Pop-Tarts? Do they still make Pop-Tarts?"

"Yes, they still make Pop-Tarts."

"Good. Pop-Tarts would be great."

He smiled. "That's no problem. Pop-Tarts it is. Anything else?"

"How about some fruit?" she said, looking at the apple.

"What kind of fruit do you like?"

"Apples are good. I like apples."

"Apples keep pretty well, too."

"And candy?" she asked.

"Candy? Like what?"

"Chocolate. Anything Chocolate."

"Okay," he said. "Pop-Tarts, apples and candy it is. Breakfast of Champions." He paused. "I'll be back tomorrow night. What time should I come?"

"I don't have a way to keep time. What time do the lights go out?"

"Ten o'clock."

"Will you come before or after the lights go out?"

"After," he said.

"Okay."

Exhibit Seven: Conception, Part II

Eddie walked inside and found Brad sitting at the security desk.

"That's it," Brad said. "The smokers are up to dinner, the administration went home and all we have left are some rounds to do later. Bea will come back down for one last smoke for the evening, but you don't really even have to watch her. I'll show you the rounds at about eight o'clock."

The security desk computer was equipped with feeds from surveillance cameras that were located at the front and rear entrances of the hospital. However, as Brad explained, the computer was mostly used to surf the Internet and play games in order to pass the time. With nothing to do for the next three hours, Eddie settled into the chair next to the desk and watched Brad plug around on the computer. It didn't take long for Eddie to get bored, and he began to daydream again.

When Eddie was twelve years old, he made his last effort to please Walter. That year, as Father's Day was approaching, Eddie thought he would do something really special for his father. When he got home from school, he found Maria alone in the kitchen. "Maria?" Eddie whispered, motioning that he wanted to talk privately.

Maria matched his tone: "Yes, Eddie?"

"I was thinking I would draw Dad a picture for Father's Day." Eddie was always a creative and imaginative little fellow, another trait that separated him from his brothers. He liked to daydream. He would wander around the woods and lake by himself, imagining scenarios of all kinds. Sometimes he was the hero; sometimes he was the victim. Eddie also excelled in his art classes at school, and he would spend hours drawing in his notebook.

"A really big picture of the lake," Eddie told Maria, full of enthusiasm. "Do you think he would like that?"

Maria hesitated. She could see the excitement in his eyes and his innocent intentions, and she knew it wouldn't turn out as he hoped. "I don't know, Eddie. Sometimes it's hard to tell with your father, although it's a good idea."

Eddie couldn't be dissuaded. He would draw Walter a picture of the lake because his father spent a lot of time there, and he hoped Walter would remember the lake more from his picture, not from the times he took Matt and Dan fishing. It would be big and beautiful, and his father would be in awe of it because nobody had ever given him such a nice gift before. His imagination ran wild while he worked on the project.

Every day after school, Eddie took a sketchpad and colored pencils down to the lake and sat on the dock and drew and drew. He imagined Walter being so impressed with the picture that he would become Walter's favorite son and they would go fishing together and do all sorts of other fun things together, while Matt and Dan would have to watch from a distance.

Eddie finished his drawing only a few days before Father's day, and he brought it inside to show Maria.

"That's beautiful, Eddie," Maria said. "Walter will love it!"

Eddie beamed.

Eddie and Maria went to the store and returned with a dark, wooden frame. Eddie ran his fingers along the edges and felt the grain of the wood with his fingertips. "This will be perfect," he said, smiling. "Thanks, Maria!"

"You're welcome, dear. Now, get that wrapped before your Dad gets home."

Maria helped Eddie wrap the drawing and tuck it safely under his bed, out of view. When they heard Walter's footsteps on the floor above their heads, they exchanged smiles as if to say, *Just in time.*

As Eddie and Maria walked up the stairs together, they heard a commotion in the dining room. Matt and Dan were talking to Walter. They stopped to listen.

"Today, we had to write a paper about what we want to be when we grow up and why," Dan said.

"We both wrote about the same thing," Matt said.

"Really?" Walter perking up. "What was it?"

"We both said we want to be dentists," Dan announced.

"We both said we want to be dentists because we want be like you, Dad," Matt added.

"And we both got an 'A.'"

"Wow," Walter said. "Here, let's put these on the refrigerator. You both want to be dentists, 'ey?"

"Of course we do," Matt replied.

Walter said, "This is the best Father's Day gift I could ever ask for."

Eddie turned and ran down the stairs, leaving Maria aghast. He didn't give Walter the drawing that day. He didn't care about it anymore.

The next night, Eddie went through the motions at the family dinner. When he was finished, he went upstairs to his room to be alone. He shut the door and flopped down on his bed. Moments later, he heard faint shuffling of feet and whispers outside his door. He got down on his knees and put his ear to the door, holding his breath to prevent making a noise. The voice sounded like Maria's, but he could only pick out a few fuzzy words.

She said something like: "Your son… Father's Day… Your son… drawing… Your son…"

There was a long silence followed by the sound of Maria leaving hallway.

Eddie's mind raced. *You might as well just give it to me straight. He's yours. The test came back positive. He's yours. Yes, it was positive. He's yours. How certain are you? I couldn't be more certain. He's yours. That's good news, isn't it? He's yours.*

Everything converged and suddenly made sense. *We want to be just like you.* He didn't rub Walter the wrong way. Melissa did. In looks, personality and interests, Eddie took after his mother, while Dan and Matt looked and acted just like their father. *This is the best gift Father's Day gift I could ever ask for.* Walter had suspected Eddie wasn't his child, and Walter had him tested. It was too late for reconciliation by that point. Walter would never view Eddie the same way he viewed Matt and Dan. Eddie was his mother's son. And, to Walter, that's what he would always be, his *mother's* son.

As the memory concluded, Eddie looked at his watch to see how much time had elapsed: seven minutes. *This is going to be a long evening,* he thought, sighing aloud.

#

Brad was now playing a computer game while Eddie looked over his shoulder. It was a first-person shooter game that gave you points for killing a non-descript enemy. The only way to tell who was on your team and who was the enemy was by the uniform. Your team was dressed in green, and the enemy was dressed in red. You could get more points for shooting the enemy in the head because it was an instant kill.

Without looking away from the game, Brad said, "Feel free, you know, to find some way to entertain yourself during these times. You can check your email or play games or whatever. I usually keep the cameras up on the screen. That way you can make sure the Administrators haven't come back for some reason, especially Stan. He's our boss. If you see a big, fat-assed, sweaty guy walking around wearing a green blazer, that's him. You can't miss him. When he's gone, you're good to go."

In the downtime, Eddie's daydream with the Volleyball Player began to evolve. He imagined running away with her to a quaint, little town near a lake, where they would live deliberately, and he would write. He imagined a small cottage with a big living room where the ceiling was open up to the second floor, and there was a loft overhead. He pictured huge bay windows open to a view of the trees and the lake with natural light bouncing about their shoulders as they went about their daily routines. It was perfect. There he could get lots of work done.

Eddie imagined one summer evening, while the Volleyball Player was sitting out on the patio drinking a mojito, he announced, "My novel is finished." As he said this, he dropped a weighty stack of papers down on the table.

"Damn it, Eddie," the Volleyball Player cursed, jumping up from her seat. "You spilled my drink."

Eddie ran to get a towel. While he mopped up the mess, the Volleyball Player said, "My goodness, Eddie, how long have you been working on this?"

"Several months now."

"What's it about, klutz?" she teased.

"It's about a man and a woman who fall in love."

"A man and a woman who fall in love? Gee, I don't think they've made that one into a movie yet."

"It's more complicated than that."

"Let me guess," she continued, "there's some reason the two lovers can't be lovers, but they will stop at nothing to be together. And it makes them do crazy things. Is that it?"

Eddie looked at the manuscript. "Sort of," he said. "But it's different."

"You better make sure Shakespeare is okay with that, Romeo, before you go publishing it. At least tell me if it's a comedy or a tragedy. Do they get married or do they die in the end?"

Eddie shrugged...

#

When it was time, Brad showed Eddie "the rounds." The rounds consisted of locking doors on the first floor, turning off the "Muzak" that was playing throughout the building. Eddie hadn't even noticed it until Brad turned it off. Brad then showed Eddie how to lock up the kitchen, which was located in the basement, and finally led him to the back entrance of the building. "That's pretty much everything," Brad said, "but there is just one more thing we have to do. Do you get spooked easily?"

"Why?" Eddie asked, getting a little spooked.

Brad stepped outside and held the back door open, waiting for Eddie to follow him. "It's not that big of a deal. We have to do some things out in the boiler room. Some people get a little scared being alone out there."

"I'll be okay," Eddie said. *I'm screwed*, he thought.

The boiler room to which Brad was referring was actually a large, brick building behind the hospital. It was three stories high, and each story had large windows that looked like tic-tac-toe boards. Several windowpanes were broken or missing. The glass that was still intact was gray with condensation, and several windows were leaking steam. The surrounding lawn was overrun with weeds and sprinkled with random pieces of garbage - candy wrappers, plastic bags and metal shards. The boiler room looked more like an abandoned warehouse than anything else.

Brad and Eddie had to cross the employee parking lot to get to it. From a distance, Eddie could see a complicated network of metal pipes and steel machinery through the windows. He led Eddie along the side of the building. "First of all, you have to walk around the building to look for anything that might be out of place." He stopped near a vent at the bottom of the sidewall where a generous gust of hot air was flowing out. "Basically, you're checking for homeless people hiding out by the steam vent. It's not a problem right now, but we get them quite frequently in the winter time."

Eddie stopped and stared at the steam flowing out of the building. He pictured a poor man huddled up there at night, holding his hands to the vent as if it was a campfire. Eddie shook the image out of his head and hurried to catch up with Brad. "What do you do if you find someone there?"

"Make them go away. If they don't, tell them you'll call the cops. They'll usually go then, but if that doesn't work, just call the cops. I've never had to do that."

The image of the poor man returned to Eddie's head, and he saw a security guard forcing the man onward. *I don't think I could do that*, he thought.

Brad stopped at a rusty, metal door with a sign posted on it that read:

DANGER
HIGH VOLTAGE
AUTHORIZED PERSONNEL ONLY

Brad unhooked a ring of keys from his belt and unlocked the door, and he stepped into a dark stairwell. Eddie followed, stepping over the threshold one foot at a time, praying for solid ground with each step. Inside, he could see a set of stairs leading downward and another set of stairs leading upwards into the darkness.

Eddie heard several piercing clicks that sounded like gunshots. He ducked and jumped backwards out of the open door.

"Sorry, dude," Brad said, laughing. He continued to flip switches inside the door, and one by one, lights came on. "I thought you said you don't spook easily."

"I usually don't," Eddie said. "I don't know what I was thinking."

"It's not a big deal, man. I used to get spooked in here too."

The lights revealed dirty, cinderblock walls lined with pipes, and for the first time Eddie noticed the horrible, musty smell. As Brad led him down the stairs into the boiler room, Eddie was reminded of "The Cask of Amontillado." Brad was surely his Montresor leading him to his imminent death.

"We have to check some gauges," Brad explained.

Yeah, check some gauges, Eddie replied in his head. *More like slay me to death. But what reasons could Brad possibly have for killing me? Maybe he doesn't need reasons. Maybe he kills people just for fun, like that computer game he was playing. Maybe that's why this job is always available!* Eddie scanned Brad's shadowy figure for a possible weapon, then shook his head in an attempt to physically debunk the ridiculous notion.

"You only have to do this if you're working second shift. The maintenance guys will do it on first shift." Brad looked at Eddie over his shoulder.

At the bottom of the stairs, Brad turned and walked through another rusty metal door identical to the one on the front of the building. Eddie hesitated to follow, but what other choice did he have? He moved through the door, and as he did so a wall of hot air greeted him. The temperature in the room was at least ten degrees warmer. The room contained three huge boiler tanks connected by a maze of pipes, and the noise they generated was deafening. It forced Brad to shout.

At the bottom of the stairs Brad stopped at a desk cluttered with dusty papers. "When you come down here, get the second shift log from the desk. This gives you a list of all the gauges to check." Brad pushed some of the papers around, then picked up a folder that was labeled "Second Shift Log." He held it up so Eddie could see it.

Eddie nodded. He was relieved to see that there was a second shift log and that gauges actually needed to be checked.

Brad opened up the folder and showed Eddie what a completed page looked like as he positioned himself in front of boiler number one. "Okay, boiler one, gauge one," he yelled, pointing at the page. "See the gauge up near the top? That's gauge one. Just write down the number. It seems to be around eighty-five. Gauge two: ninety-seven. And gauge three: ninety-four. You don't need to know what they mean. Just write down the number."

Brad repeated the same procedure for the other two tanks. As Brad checked the last gauge on the last tank, a violent noise pierced the room. "Cover!" Brad shouted and ducked behind the desk. Eddie dove to the floor and covered his head.

Eddie didn't hear the noise stop; it was ringing in his head. He felt something hit his shoulder, and he shrieked.

"Eddie," Brad yelled, shaking him by the shoulder. "Eddie! It's me, Brad. It's okay. It was only the air valve release."

Eddie rolled over and uncovered his eyes to see Brad standing over him.

Brad nearly fell over he was laughing so hard. He said, "Sorry, man. I didn't mean to scare you. Loud noises have made me jumpy ever since I was in Iraq."

Eddie's terror turned to embarrassment. His shirt was drenched with heavy amounts of sweat that was pouring down his forehead, neck and back.

"Are you alright? You hit the deck pretty hard."

"Yeah, I'm alright. I guess it is pretty spooky down here."

"You'll get used to it," Brad said. He put the second shift log back on the desk and headed up the stairs.

"Is that all we have to do?" asked Eddie.

"No, we still have to walk through the rooms upstairs."

Eddie didn't ask why. He was afraid to know the answer.

Brad stopped when he reached the second floor. "There are mostly storage rooms up here. This is where the maintenance guys store a bunch of junk."

Brad walked down the first hallway, briefly peeking into each room. Eddie followed and looked to see what was being stored. One room contained shelves full of paint cans and paint brushes, another room was piled high with dirty old blankets and other stained linens, and another room was filled with random scraps of wood and other metals.

Who thought it was a good idea to save this crap? Eddie wondered.

They walked back to the top of the stairs and continued the same process down the opposite hallway. "To be honest, we're looking for people," Brad mentioned casually. "Some homeless people might try to sneak in here and set up camp. We got that jail across the way. When they release people, they'll give them a buck or two for bus fair and kick them out the front door. Sometimes we get some pretty shady characters around here, and if they don't have a place to go, they might try to hide out in here. I guess it's happened before."

Eddie could see the Police Department and the jailhouse from a window as they peeked into another room. *Why, God*? Eddie demanded. *Why couldn't I have gotten a real job?*

In the corner of the last room, there was a ladder attached to the wall that led up through a hole in the ceiling. Eddie didn't want to know what it was, but the fear of the unknown persuaded him. "What's up there?"

"That's the attic. I don't think there's even anything up there." Brad turned and headed back toward the stairway. "That's all. Let's go."

Brad turned off the lights and locked the door as they left, and they returned to the main building. Eddie was comforted by the sterile scent of the nursing home. It somehow signified safety now. He was content to sit in his chair next to the security desk watching Brad gun down enemies on the computer, because anything was better than thinking about re-entering that boiler room again, alone.

Two

"Where did you go?" she asked.

"I wanted to check something," he replied.

She continued eating.

"I guess I should've brought more food."

"I'm sorry. I'll slow down. I'm so hungry."

"I know. It's late to have dinner."

"..."

"I brought Hershey's for chocolate," he said. "I hope that's okay."

"..."

"And bread, peanut butter, crackers and cheese."

"..."

"And water."

"Thank you so much."

"They didn't have Pop-Tarts."

"That's fine."

"I will get them for you next time."

"Don't worry about it," she said. "For a while, I thought you might stand me up."

"I said I'd be here."

"I know. It's just...I haven't always had the greatest luck."

"Why are you..." He stopped.

She eyed him.

"I mean, what do you..."

"..."

"Where are you from?" he asked at last.

"Around here. That's all you need to know."

"I'm sorry," he said. "Have you been seeing anyone else?"

"No. Nobody." She broke off some cheese, pushed it into a ball of bread and popped it into her mouth. She chewed for some time, then said, "They might not be as nice to me as you are."

"You are lucky I saw you before someone else did. I think you'll be fine here for a while, if you're careful."

She smiled.

"How did you find this place?"

She ignored the question.

"I only ask because I want to know if you can get in and out of here easily."

"Yes, I can. One of the basement windows is broken."

"Good. Which one?"

"I didn't break it," she said.

" … "

"The one on the backside. The one mostly hidden by bushes."

"I noticed the front door can be locked and unlocked from the inside. That is an option, but the door is noisy. We better use the window."

"Sure."

"Later tonight, I'll drop off a bag down by the window. Be sure to pick it up right away before someone else finds it. Be careful. Make sure nobody sees you."

She nodded. "If it's not too much trouble…"

"What is it?"

"A flashlight."

"Of course. I didn't even think about that."

"I, you know, won't be able to repay you," she said, averting her eyes.

"I'm happy to. Really."

"Thank you."

Exhibit Eight: Persistence

Eddie slipped quickly and easily into the ebb and flow of life at Fifth Street Community Hospital, and he experienced a significant change in his attitude and in his quality of life. In the months preceding his employment, he was aware of and saddened by the ever-widening communication gap between him and his friends from college. In recent weeks, the frequency of those thoughts had decreased and his self-esteem and sense of fulfillment had improved. He found himself looking forward to his shifts every day and he began putting on his uniform with a sense of pride. He even felt, to some extent, that he was somehow destined for that ordinary position in order to do extraordinary things, whatever that might be.

One day, after Eddie punched in and relieved Brad of his post, he noticed that Shirley was extra cheerful. "How come you are so happy today?" asked Eddie.

"I'm all out of smokes," Shirley said in her thick southern accent. She adjusted her frail body to a position more suited for conversation.

"You're out of smokes?" Eddie said. "Why are you so happy about that?"

"My son's going to bring me some more smokes today. He works at the airport. He says he's going to stop by on his way home and drop some off."

"That's nice."

Shirley's attitude changed unexpectedly, and she said, "That's the least he can do, seeing as how he hardly ever has time to stop by, let alone take me anywhere. He says he's too busy with my granddaughter's equestrian team - you know, with the horses."

Eddie knew; Shirley had told him several times before. She continued as if she was telling him for the first time, "It seems like she's always got something going on with that, but I says to him, 'When can I come watch?' He says it wouldn't work with the horses and all, but I know he doesn't bring the horses around by himself, if he even helps haul the horses at all. You know? And I don't think my granddaughter has those events as much as he says she does."

"I'm sorry to hear that."

"Yeah, well," she said, sinking back into her wheelchair. "He says he's coming today."

During the post-lunch lull, Eddie's fantasy continued. He imagined selling the book for a humble advance and seeing the novel appear in stores in time for Christmas. It was a mysterious little book, black with a silhouette of a security guard in an open doorway on the cover. From the doorway, the security guard's flashlight was shining light into a dark room, highlighting letters along the bottom that read: *Troubled Waters.* A novel by E.W. Waters.

"They want me to go on tour," Eddie told The Volleyball Player one day. "Go to bookstores all over and do readings."

"Do you have to?"

"I should, if I want the book to make money."

"We have a good thing going here, Eddie. I don't want you to be gone all the time."

"This is something I have to do. I have to promote my book."

They didn't have time to talk it through before Eddie left for the book tour...

"God*damn* it!" yelled Bob, bursting through the front door. He shuffled along the sidewalk as fast as his one good leg and one good arm could move him. The onlookers, startled by the eruption, watched as Bob scooted into his spot between Sam and Bea.

"What's the matter with you now, Bob?" asked Sam.

"It's this goddamned administration again."

"Hey now, watch that language of yours," Bea said.

Bob ignored Bea and continued, "Now they're telling me I can't have snacks in between meals. My daughter brought me some candy bars yesterday and they stole them." Bob pounded his fist on the armrest of his chair.

"I know," Sam said in his calm, bored manner. "They took away my potato chips yesterday. I just bought them too. The nurse aides came in and took them right out of my hand. And later, I saw the same bag of chips in the trash at the nurses' station. Someone ate my chips. I know they did."

Bob grumbled and pounded his fist again. David began laughing uncontrollably, spilling saliva down the front of his shirt.

"What you laughing at?" Bob demanded.

David recoiled, slurping. He looked at Eddie and mumbled, mimicking Bob's fist pounding.

"Leave him alone, Bob," Bea said. "You're not mad at him." Bea turned to Eddie and explained, "Bob's had some trouble with his wife stealing from him, and now he thinks everyone's out to get him."

"Don't you ever get sick of the way they treat us around here?" Bob asked Bea.

"Of course I do. I'm old, but I'm not that old. I can still decide what I want to eat when I want to eat it, and

I don't need any administrator telling me that." Bea lit another cigarette.

"Amen, sister," Sam agreed.

"That's all I'm saying," Bob said. "They're treating me like a child. Pretty soon we won't have any rights around here."

"Bob had a fortune," Bea said, addressing Eddie as if they were alone. "His father started a successful chain of general stores, and Bob loved those stores. He worked hard and expanded the business. Things were going fine until Bob had his stroke. When he was in the hospital, his wife paid some crooked doctor and lawyer to arrange for Bob to sign all his possessions over to her along with the final say in all his healthcare decisions. Now, he's got nothing, and he has to stay here unless his wife agrees to let him out. Sad, I know, but I think Bob secretly prefers to be here with us." Bea smiled at Bob.

"It ain't so bad," Bob admitted. "If they take away our smokes, that'll be the end of it."

"They still...won't...let me...smoke," David added.

"Smoking's no good for you, boy," Sam said. "Smoking's what got you into this mess to begin with."

David looked to Eddie and said, "They won't...let me...smoke."

"No, they won't," Shirley said. "When I first met David, he asked me for a cigarette, and I asked him if he could have one, and he said he could, so I gave him one. Then, they took it away from him because he can't have them, and I got in trouble. They tried to take away my smoking privileges too, because of it. So, next time he asked me for one, I said no, and he called me a little bitch."

David smiled at Eddie and repeated, "Little bitch..."

"See," Shirley said.

Eddie nodded.

Bob wheeled himself out of his spot and down the sidewalk. As he passed Sam, he said, "Let's go down to the patio. We need to talk." Sam followed Bob without hesitation, and the two of them slowly made their way down to the patio. They settled into a shaded area with their backs facing Eddie and the others began to talk enthusiastically.

"They're planning to escape," Bea said. "They've been planning it for years. They think nobody knows what they're talking about, but they don't hide it very well."

"Where are they planning to go?" asked Eddie.

"Who knows where they're planning to go, but nowhere is where they're going to go." Bea chuckled. "You boys better finish up your secret society meeting pretty quick," she shouted toward the patio. "I'm going to come down there to water my flowers in a minute."

Eddie paced the sidewalk to keep his legs loose, counting the cracks as he passed over them.

"Did I ever tell you about the time when my daddy whipped my sister good?" Shirley said.

In two weeks, Eddie could recite the story better than Shirley, but he stopped pacing to listen to her tell it again. "What happened, Shirley?"

"My sister had a friend who lived two hills over and my daddy told her, 'You can have your friend over anytime you want, but I don't want you playing over there.' But my sister did it anyway. When she came back, he yelled at her, 'You git over here.' But she acted like she didn't hear him. That night, my daddy whipped her good, and she said she'd never do it again. When we asked him why she couldn't go to her friend's house but she could come to our house, he said, 'All they do is drink and gamble and party over there, and I don't want you girls around that.' And then we understood him. And my sister never went to play at her friend's house ever again, but she came over to our house whenever she wanted." Shirley took a long drag from her cigarette, then added, "My daddy was tough, but he was fair."

Bea produced a water bottle from the bag hanging off of the back of her chair. She moved to the corner of the building and shouted, "Ready or not, here I come." She released her wheels and let the slope of the sidewalk propel her toward the patio. Bob glared over his shoulder as she approached.

Bea's flowers looked more like three weeds poking up through the woodchips around the patio. She brought her chair to a stop at the edge of the bricks and carefully poured an estimated one-third of the water at the root of each green stem. When she was finished, she sat up and looked lovingly upon her scraggily weeds.

"When are you going to give up on them anyhow?" asked Bob. "It's July, you know."

"The seasons are changing slowly this year. It's not too late." Bea turned her chair and began to roll herself back up the sidewalk.

Eddie soon discovered that life at the Fifth Street Community Hospital ran on routine and regularity. Around five o'clock, same time every day, a group of nurse aides made their way down to retrieve the residents for dinner. Shirley pleaded with the aide that approached her, "Can I just stay a little longer? I'm waiting for my son to bring me some cigarettes."

"You have to come up for your dinner now," the aide said. "Your food is ready."

"I'm not even hungry."

"You know you have to eat something, and you have to take your medication."

"Let me wait for fifteen more minutes."

The other aides proceeded to wheel the rest of the residents inside. On the way, Bob offered Shirley some support. "Just let her stay for fifteen more god*damned* minutes. What the hell are you paid for anyhow?"

To Shirley, the aide said, "You have to come now. I'm not coming back down to get you."

"Would it be okay," Eddie said, "if she waited for fifteen more minutes? I'll bring her up."

The nurse aide scowled, shocked that the security guard would undermine her authority. "I guess that would be okay," she said. The aide relocked Shirley's brakes. "Only for fifteen minutes."

"Thank you," Eddie said.

The aide said nothing and marched back into the building.

Now Eddie was as anxious as Shirley was for her son to show up. Together, they scrutinized every car that drove past the hospital for the next fifteen minutes. Hope came and went with each one.

At last, Shirley said, "You can take me up now."

"I'm sorry, Shirley."

Shirley grunted and hung her head low as Eddie wheeled her into the building.

Three

"Marilyn?" he called.

"Yes?"

"I found more blankets downstairs."

"Won't someone notice them missing?"

"I doubt it. These were unopened. From 2005 even. These rooms are for storage, but I don't think anyone uses them anymore."

"Oh, thank God. That's wonderful!"

"How is the sandwich? Do you like turkey and cheese?"

"It's delicious. Thank you very much."

"I made it myself."

"I see that," she said, between bites.

"So, tell me more about you? What's your family like?"

She stopped chewing.

"I'm sorry," he said. "You don't have to answer that."

"No, it's fine. I'm sorry."

"It's okay. You don't have to…"

"I would prefer not to talk about my family. I had a bad experience. It was my horrible step-father."

"It's okay," he said. "I don't want to talk about family either. How about we skip that topic for now?"

"Sure."

"I was a nerd as a kid."

"Nerdy how?"

"I liked to read a lot. Being a boy, you're not supposed to like to read. You have to do boy stuff. Play sports and blow stuff up. I would hideout in my room whenever I could be alone and lose myself in the stories."

She smiled.

"I would have loved this place."

"…"

"As a hideout. As a kid."

"I was nerdy too," she said. "More dorky really. I used to be this prissy, girly-girl, cheerleader type. I was popular too, until…"

"What?"

"Until I left high school."

"Were you any good as a cheerleader? Did you do a lot of flips or whatever?"

"Yeah, I was good. As good as anybody could be at cheerleading. I was the captain of the varsity team as a sophomore."

"Did you do competitions and stuff like that?"

"Some pretty lame ones, I guess. We mostly stood around in skimpy skirts and yelled cheesy chants at the boys' games. It's embarrassing now. I was really into it back then."

"That's funny," he said. "I can kind of see that about you."

"At least I wasn't a nerd. Tell me, when did that stop?"

"Alright, you got me there. What year did you graduate?"

"I, um…"

"I'm sorry. I just assumed you…"

"Wait a minute. First, you're going to suggest I don't have what it takes to be a good cheerleader, and now you're asking me how old I am? You really know how to talk to the ladies, don't you?"

"I didn't mean to."

"I'm just teasing you," she said.

"But you're right, talking to girls has not been my strong suit."

"Yes, I can see that. You were the kind of kid that didn't need Halloween to dress up like a character from a book. Not exactly a turn-on."

"Weird, I know," he said, standing up. "I'm sorry, but I have to get going. Stay out of trouble now. And try to resist the temptation to cheer for me as I leave."

"Oh, ha-ha, funnyman. Just get out of my space, you nerd."

Exhibit Nine: Restriction

Working at the nursing home, Eddie became aware of several fundamental problems in the way the place operated. The administration constantly created new policies and procedures that often limited the residents' freedoms in order to make things *easier*. From their comfortable chairs, behind their large desks, in offices off-limits to the residents, they ruled the hospital like kings in distant castles, isolated from any sort of personal contact with the general population. The administrators seemed to ignore the common resident's plight in lieu of a vague conception of *greater good*. The administration's decision, for example, to limit the residents' access to snacks between meals happened without explanation. Immediately this new policy became the issue of utmost concern, and every employee was instructed to be on the lookout for snacking renegades that might stir up a rebellion by opening a bag of potato chips in the afternoon.

New rules and regulations, like the Snack Rule, were mysteriously passed down an unknown chain of command until they reached the most common staff members - groundskeepers, janitors, nurse aides, receptionists, volunteers and, of course, security guards. These were the people expected to carry out the new commands. For Eddie, this meant getting a call from Stan, who was almost always eating something himself. He would say, between bites, something that invariably began: "The folks upstairs want you to make sure the resident's don't *blah blah blah*..." Because most of the requests were absurd, Eddie tried to avoid answering the phone all together.

One time he answered the phone and a high-pitched voice squeaked through the receiver: "Yes, security? How come I see a resident in front of the building eating from a bag of pretzels?"

Eddie was stunned by the angry tone of the unknown caller. From the desk he scanned the courtyard and saw Bob sitting out on the patio, who was, in fact, enjoying a bag of pretzels. "What do you mean?" asked Eddie.

"Aren't you aware of the new Snack Rule?" the woman snapped.

"Yes, of course." Eddie tried to sound as genuine as he could. "The residents are only allowed to have a snack in between meals. I'm sorry. I'll bring him inside right away." He hung up the phone and waited to see if the woman would call back. She did. Eddie answered the phone. "Hello? Security Desk. This is Eddie. How may I be of assistance to you?"

The woman's voice grew whinier and more annoying with each word. "Yes. I just called. Did you say you were going to bring him inside?"

"Yes, ma'am," Eddie said. "I'm going to bring him right in. I'm on my way out there right now."

"That's not the new rule about snacking." She was nearly shouting. "The residents aren't allowed to eat anything in between meals!"

"Right. They're not allowed to eat in, between meals."

"What?"

"That's why he's outside." Eddie was pleased with himself.

"No. He's not allowed to eat anything in between meals anywhere!"

"Oh, I'm sorry," Eddie said, trying hard not to laugh. "I must have misinterpreted the message from Stan."

"The residents aren't allowed to eat between meals," she repeated. "Please go remind that resident and properly dispose of the contraband."

"The resident has contraband as well?" Eddie asked.

"No. The pretzels are the contraband."

"Right, right, right. Okay. I'm on it." Eddie hung up the phone.

He walked outside, sat down on the bench near Bob and said, "The people upstairs are still pushing that Snack Rule."

Bob glared at him and clutched the bag of pretzels close to his side. "You can take the pretzels out of my cold dead hands."

"I know. I know," Eddie said. "I don't want to take them from you, but if I don't it's going to be my ass. I'm hoping we can make a deal."

"I'm listening," Bob said without taking his eyes off Eddie.

"You give me your pretzels, so the folks up stairs will see that I took care of it."

"No!" Bob shouted, stuffing the pretzel bag down into his chair next to him.

"I'll put some of your pretzels in a small, plastic baggy and give them back to you, but you'll have to make sure you eat them secretly. That way I can keep my job and you can keep your pretzels." Eddie waited for a response, but Bob didn't answer. "Do it for me, Bob. Work with me here."

For a moment, Bob didn't move. Then, lowering his head in a heart-breaking gesture of shame and defeat, he extended the bag toward Eddie and released the pretzels. Eddie took the bag and scampered inside before Bob could change his mind.

The Ziploc bags in the bottom drawer of the security desk were used to package the residents' cigarette cartons when they weren't smoking. The cartons were bagged, tagged and alphabetized in the top drawer. Eddie distributed the pretzels into several Ziploc bags and labeled them "Bob's" in permanent marker. He set one bag aside and put the rest in the cigarette drawer next to Bob's cigarettes. When he returned to the patio, he pretended to be comforting Bob in the loss of his snack while he dropped the bag onto Bob's lap.

"Them bastards try to take everything from us."

"I know. I know. Thanks for helping me out, Bob."

#

In the circle of life, people are given a curfew at a young age for reasons of safety - to prevent adolescent misbehaviors and to protect the sanity of the parents and the community. Once the curfew is lifted, people enjoy many years of so-called freedom. However, as people get older, the curfews get set back into place - either naturally, by the fatigue of old age, or by force - for we cannot have the evening streets crowded with elderly misfits and geriatric hooligans who might do any number of outrageous and awful crimes. Perhaps this is intended to signify the coming of the end - the nearly completed revolution of life's circle. Whatever the reason the residents at the Fifth Street Community Hospital were not allowed outside after nine-thirty.

On most evenings, after Eddie finished the rounds, Bea would come back down to enjoy one or two more cigarettes before being forced to retire. He enjoyed the evenings with Bea. She was still a competent conversationalist and a wonderful storyteller. In those quiet and peaceful moments at dusk, she was more than happy to share any of the residents' life stories with Eddie. She knew more details about her fellow residents than they could remember themselves, and she told their tales as if she was reading them word for word out of a short-story collection.

"How long has David been here?" Eddie asked one night.

"A while now. Two years. He's here serving a life-time sentence for idiocy."

"What?" Eddie was caught off guard by Bea's unusually frank response.

"Yes," she said. "As the story goes, David had a fight with his girlfriend, like usual. He was partying with some buddies, and they were keeping David's son awake. She was pregnant again, and she couldn't handle it, so she kicked him and his buddies out of the house. They all went out to the garage to drink and smoke and carry on. Eventually, one of his buddies had the brilliant idea to go snowmobiling - it was winter at the time. David was too wasted to think straight. The accident was inevitable.

"David was in the snow for six hours before he was discovered, and for some reason, by some slim chance, against all odds, he survived. After twelve surgeries and three weeks in a medically-induced coma, David woke up. His brain was there, but - well, you know.

"When David came to, he was introduced to his second son, who was already one week old. After extensive rehab, they moved him here. He was told by his family and their doctor that he would stay only until his speech and motor skills improved. The doctors felt it was best not to discourage him with the truth." Bea rolled her eyes. "Now, two years later, David is still here. Visits from his family members are few and far between. His girlfriend only brings the kids around on special occasions. She avoids all his questions about marriage. I can't blame her. His friends visited at first, but the guilt was too much. They probably don't even call David to tell him why they don't come around anymore." Bea took one last puff of her cigarette and dropped the butt into the Safe-Smoker ashtray.

"That's so sad," Eddie said, not knowing what else to say.

"Yes, it is. I've been in a wheel chair for a long time, and I've lived here for even longer. My youthful days came, I enjoyed them and now they're long gone. I try to enjoy what I have left where I am, but David missed his best days." Bea unlocked her wheels and rolled herself toward the door. "He'll be here long after I'm gone. Good night, Eddie."

Four

"I brought you some wine this time, per your request," he said.

"What kind?"

"A white wine. That's what you said, right?"

"I don't think I asked for anything specific," she said. "I'm not really a wine drinker. I just thought it would be nice, you know, to have some alcohol. How do you open it?"

"Damn, I didn't even think of that."

"It's okay. We'll figure something out. Homeless people manage to do it somehow. We can come up with something." She stuck the butt end of a plastic fork down into the cork and tried to leverage it out. The fork snapped. "Okay, that didn't work. Here, try to push it down into the bottle."

He took a mini flashlight out of his chest pocket and pressed the handle down on the cork. The cork resisted, then gave way. When it released, he almost fell over backwards.

"It worked! I knew you could do it." She squeezed his bicep.

He poured two red Solo cups half full. "To prosperity," he said, holding his glass up for a toast.

"To freedom," she replied, and they drank. "It's kind of sour, isn't it?"

"I don't drink wine much. It tastes like a funny grape juice to me."

"This is nice," she said.

"Yes, it's nice."

"Tell me, what do you want to be when you grow up?"

"Don't you mean, what did I want to be when I was growing up? I'm all grown up now."

"You mean, you didn't want to be a...what are you?"

"Technically, I'm a security guard, but I'm really a babysitter...an elderly-sitter, actually. My job is to watch residents smoke. Every elderly person with a cigarette is a potential arsonist, you know. They're a liability. I don't even work for the hospital. I work for a security company. The hospital outsources the job so they don't have to pay me well or provide me with benefits or anything. I'm living my dream."

"It's better than the gig I got going on," she said. "The uniform is much better."

"I'm a rent-a-cop."

"Don't sell yourself short."

"I wish I wasn't selling myself at all."

"I think you look handsome. In the uniform, that is. Women like a man in uniform."

"Not all uniforms."

"I like your badge."

"You're ridiculous," he said. "What about you? You've got to be one of the best dressed homeless chicks around, especially in the clothes I bought you."

"Now you're being ridiculous. What do you come in here for anyways?" she asked, changing the subject.

He choked on his wine.

"Why do you come in the building?" she said. "Not why you come to see me, silly. I know that."

"I have to do some paperwork downstairs, but I'm not even sure what I'm supposed to be looking for, and I really don't care. I just pretend and try to get through each day, hoping nobody will notice."

"I understand that," she said.

"I know you know."

"I feel like I can talk to you. There's just something about you. You seem, you know, real."

"Well, I don't have any reason to be anything but humble," he said.

"Ha! I'll drink to that."

"Want some more?"

"Yes, please."

"What about you?" he asked, filling her glass. "Is this what you dreamed of doing when you were a child?"

"No, of course not," she said. "I never thought I'd be here. And I never thought I'd be doing this. I never even thought I'd be drinking wine even. My step-father was a horrible man; he was an alcoholic. Everyone loved him so much and thought he was so great. Sorry, I know we weren't going to talk about that."

"It's okay. You can talk about whatever you want, but you don't have to talk about anything either."

"He was abusive. My mom had her own problems. I don't blame her. It wasn't her fault. She didn't even know. I was helpless, so I bottled it up inside. One day, I couldn't take it anymore. I lost control, and I..."

"..."

"I had to run away."

"That's so sad," he said.

"Well, I'm here, now. This is an improvement, if you can believe it. I was a normal kid once. I just needed to get to adulthood, but I'm not sure I'll make it now."

"I know that feeling. Trust me. Growing up with my family, there was all this pressure. My dad expected all of us kids to do everything he did."

"I take it you didn't want to do what he wanted."

"No. Definitely not. See, most kids' parents tell them, 'You can be anything you want to be when you grow up. You can do anything you put your mind to.' Stuff like that. My dad told us, 'You'll be great dentists.' I was different, though. I never wanted to be a dentist, so when I decided not to go to dental school, my dad made it very clear to me that I was on my own. At any time I could change my mind and go back, but until then I would be cut off. I guess, we're not so different, you and I."

She shook her head.

"I mean…"

"No, it's fine," she said. "Similar experiences, for sure. Different outcomes, though. If you don't mind me asking, what about your mother? Where was she in all this?"

"My mother. That's a whole different story. I think she, you know, like you said, had her own problems. I think she just couldn't figure out where her life took a wrong turn. She made all the right moves, so she thought, but her life just didn't add up as she had expected."

"Here, here." She offered her glass up and they toasted.

"I think it happens because of misguided expectations. Everybody wants lemonade, but there's not enough to go around. Some just get a little sugar. Some just get lemons."

"Ha!"

"I'm just rambling now," he said.

"And even if you get all the right parts," she added, "there's some bully ready to ruin your whole batch."

"Exactly. I don't mean to be so whiney."

"Oh, ha! Because of the wine. I get it. I think it's the wine, actually. It's making me somber, but I like it. It feels good. I haven't told anyone in years."

"I'm sorry," he said. "About all this."

"Don't be. You're doing more than enough for me."

"Is there anything else I can do?"

"You can meet me back here tomorrow. I'd like that," she said.

"I can do that. You got it."

"Can you bring me a magazine, maybe? I feel so disconnected."

"What kind?"

"*People*," she said. "You know, the gossip magazine. Do they still make it?"

"I'll bring you the latest issue."

"Oh, thank you, thank you, thank you!" She gave him a hug. "You're the best."

Exhibit Ten: Reflection

One day Eddie came into work and found Sam sitting outside all by himself. "They all went to a baseball game," Sam explained. "A group of volunteers takes them every so often."

"How come you didn't go?" asked Eddie.

"I didn't feel like going through all the fuss, getting all loaded up in the van and going through the crowds and all that. Bea gets all excited about it. She tries to get everybody to go to stuff. She sure is the youngest in the head of all of us, and she's been here the longest, too. She's used to this life."

With everyone gone, there was even more downtime than usual. Eddie lost himself in his daydreams once again. He imagined receiving a phone call one day. At first, he didn't recognize the voice on the other end of the line.

MELISSA: Eddie, this is your mother.

Eddie was speechless.

MELISSA: Eddie? Are you there?

EDDIE: Yes. I'm here.

MELISSA: How are you, dear?

EDDIE: I'm fine.

MELISSA: Eddie, we've seen you on television.

EDDIE: Yeah?

MELISSA: We've seen you promoting your book. We've seen your book too, at Schuler's even.

EDDIE: Good. Did you read it?

MELISSA: No, not yet. Your father says some parts are pretty, well, detailed. When are you coming home?

EDDIE: ...

MELISSA: Eddie, your father wants to speak with you.

EDDIE: ...

WALTER: Edward?

EDDIE: Eddie.

A long silence followed.

WALTER: So, you're a writer now?

EDDIE: I am.

WALTER: We were worried when we didn't hear from you.

EDDIE: I didn't hear from you either.

WALTER: I read your book.

EDDIE: Yes. That's what Melissa said.

WALTER: When you come home, I'd like to talk to you about it.

EDDIE: I'm not planning to return. Not anytime soon.

WALTER: What do you mean?

EDDIE: What don't you understand, Walter? What difference would it make to you?

WALTER: Eddie. I know we've had our differences.

EDDIE: Differences? You've had your differences. Now that I've been successful, living my life my way, you want something. You never wanted anything from me before, except to go away. But now you want, what? Credit? Validation? Recognition? *Money?*

WALTER: Eddie.

EDDIE: I won't give you any of that, but thank you for giving me great material. And thanks for calling. I've been waiting a long time for this conversation.

WALTER: Eddie, you're being...

Eddie hung up the phone...

Sam interrupted the silence. "Bob and I got here about the same time." He scratched his shiny, bald head with a long, slender finger. Everything about Sam was long: his head, his hands, his legs, his feet. His torso was so long he seemed unable to hold his shoulders up straight. Even his speech was long and slow. "I've been here about a year, maybe," he said. "We're roommates, you know?"

"I know," Eddie said.

"Yup. Got here at the same time, share the same room and have the same problems." Sam pointed at the limp side of his body with his good hand.

Eddie nodded.

"I'm from Detroit originally. All my family lives over there. This is the only home I could afford. The government helps us out a little bit, but not enough. Only problem is I don't get to see my family much. I just don't know what to do with all this time, you know?"

"Yeah. I understand."

"I was always working before...all the time. Couldn't afford not to. I had me a wife to look after. Couldn't ever hold down good work, though. I just hopped from one factory to the next. Always seemed to have bad luck somehow. Sometimes I couldn't find a ride to work, and they'd tell me I was in luck because I didn't have to find a ride there no more. Being able to live here is the only helping hand I've ever seen."

"Does your wife come to visit?"

"Oh, she's with me all the time. She passed years ago, but that's good. She was really spiritual, you know? Bless her heart, and I hope to see her in heaven. That's why I have to be good, you know? Just waiting my turn now. Got too much time on my hands, though. Makes me miss my family too much."

"Having too much time to think can be a bad thing," Eddie said.

"Mmm-hmm," Sam agreed.

Five

"You're early," she said, giving him a hug.

"Is this a bad time?" he asked.

"It's a bad time." She rolled her eyes.

"I was too excited to wait. I wanted to see you."

"I'm embarrassed. I'm not put together. Let me finish brushing my teeth."

"How is that working out for you? Do you like that toothbrush?"

"It's great. Sometimes you forget how good it feels just to brush your teeth and to wash your face, you know?"

"I bet."

"Do you wash your face?"

"Not usually," he admitted. "I do in the shower, I guess."

"I didn't think you'd have to. You have very clear skin. As you can see I get all..."

"You have beautiful skin."

"Thanks," she said, blushing.

He smiled.

"Alright, now, out with it. What do you have hiding behind your back?"

"You'll have to guess first."

"You really are a dork. Come on, now, out with it."

"Guess first."

"I don't want to guess. Come on."

"You come on. Guess."

"You brought me flowers!" she teased. "You're so sweet, but really, you shouldn't have. You'll spoil me."

"Nope. Not flowers. Why? Did you want flowers?"

"Come on, you nerd," she said, punching his shoulder. "We both know it's the *People* magazine I asked you to bring."

"Maybe it's a diamond ring. How about that? And, what if I'm not going to give it to you now."

"I'd rather have the magazine," she said.

"Good," he said, handing over the magazine.

"I knew it."

She browsed through the magazine while she ate. "What's all this?"

"That's a *real* treat, an exclusive interview with Paris Hilton."

"What'd she do now?"

"She's in jail."

She looked concerned.

"What?"

"Nothing. Why is she in jail?"

"I don't know. Drugs. Drinking and driving. A suspended license, maybe. It's all very important. Everyone is very concerned about her."

She studied the article for several minutes.

"What?" he asked.

"Nothing."

"Really. What?"

"Why is she so famous?"

"Because she's rich, I think."

"I don't understand people like that," she said.

"With all that money." He shook his head.

"Why do people even care about people like that?"

"She's the American dream. She's living it, and people want to see what it looks like."

"You can't live the American dream from jail."

He laughed.

"I know you can't," she said.

"I think part of it is that we're sadistic. Most people aren't beautiful and rich and famous, and we like to see when the rich fall and fall hard."

"Do you think she's beautiful?"

"Well, she's not my type."

"Really? What's your type, then?"

"…"

"Come on, what's your type?"

"I don't know."

"Don't be like that. Come on. What's your type?"

"Someone more like…"

"Like who?"

"More like you."

"Aw, you're sweet. You're a liar, but you're sweet."

"Alright, what's your type?" he asked.

"A lady doesn't kiss and tell."

"I'm not aware of any kiss. So, I guess you can…"

She leaned over and kissed him on the lips. "How about now?" she asked.

"Now that's a different story."

"I like a man in uniform."

He blushed.

"Who's this guy?" she asked, pretending the kiss was not a big deal.

"You really don't know who that is?"

"It says here he's a golfer."

"Yes, he's a golfer. The most famous golfer in the world. Probably the most famous athlete on the planet."

"Tiger Woods," she said, reading the caption. "I've heard of him. According to this, he had a baby recently."

"Now, his wife is hot."

"Down boy. She just had a baby. Wait a minute. You say she's hot, and Paris Hilton is not your type?"

"Yes. Why?"

"You have to be lying about one of them. They're, like, the same."

"No, they're not."

"What's the difference?"

"Just look at them. They're different."

"Neither of them look very much like me," she said. "Maybe that was a lie."

"Alright, now you're being…"

"I'm just teasing you. Relax. According to this article, they had a girl and named her Sam. What do you think of the name Sam for a girl?"

"I don't know. It's alright."

"I like it. I think it's cute. I hate my name. Norma…"

"What's that?" he asked.

"Nothing. I meant, I *normally* don't like guy-type names for girls. But I like that one."

"Oh."

"Do you want to have kids?" she asked.

"I think so. Eventually."

"Me too."

"Although I need to get my life straightened out before I can think about that," he added.

"Ha! Me too."

"It's getting late."

"No," she said.

"What?"

"Stay with me."

"I can't. I have to get back to work. They'll notice I'm gone. They'll get suspicious."

"Maybe this will convince you," she said, kissing him again. "What do you think now?"

"I think that was nice. I think I liked that."
"Stay. I demand it. You're staying."
"Okay, but only for a few more minutes."

Exhibit Eleven: Hallucination

Like navigating sensitive issues with the residents, Eddie learned how to manage the evening rounds without too much trouble. He developed a routine, which began by heading straight out to the boiler room. He started this habit in order to make it through the ghostly building before dark. He had, for the most part, conquered his boiler-room demons. It was not that he was no longer scared, but rather that he had gotten quite good at forcing sinister thoughts out of his head while simultaneously forcing good thoughts in. He was brainwashing himself every time he did the rounds.

Nevertheless, Eddie continued to check the gauges in considerable haste, and he often skipped checking the gauges all together by simply marking down numbers that were similar to the previous shift's numbers. He frequently rushed though the hallways upstairs without even looking into any of the rooms, hoping there wasn't anything or anyone there. He wasn't even sure why he still went through the trouble.

One Friday night, Eddie was in a hurry more than usual. It was payday, and he was hoping to do some shopping online before Bea came down after dinner. Eddie hurried down the hallway toward the back entrance of the hospital, burst through the back door and ran across the parking lot to the boiler room. To save time, he skipped the walk around the exterior of the building. If there was a problem, he would probably have a heart attack or crap himself or run away crying like a twelve-year-old girl.

That I can do without, he thought. *Stan can deal with it.*

Steam and the smell of mold greeted Eddie as he unlocked the door and stepped into the dark stairway of the boiler room. He headed down to check the gauges. At the desk he found the second-shift log, flipped it open to the first blank page and copied all the gauge readings from three days prior. He closed the folder, threw it back onto the pile of clutter and continued on his way.

As he headed back up the stairs, a voice in the back of his head warned, *If you keep doing that and something goes wrong, they might catch on to you.*

It'll be fine, he reassured himself. *I can always say I'm new and I didn't notice any problems.*

Eddie had no intention of walking through the rooms upstairs, but as he reached the door a clanging noise came from above. He froze. *What the hell was that?* All his senses were alert - survival mode code red. His eyes and ears impatiently searched for more information. *What the hell was that?*

He tried to convince himself he was alone. *That's just your imagination playing tricks on you. I'm sure it's nothing. Just walk through, and you'll see everything is fine, and you'll be on your way.* Eddie couldn't get himself to do anything. His feet were cemented to the floor. He held his breath to hear better but the sound of his racing heartbeat overwhelmed his ears.

Eddie coaxed his body into taking the first step up the stairs. He waited there for another sound as if moving six inches closer would scare the mysterious beast away.

No sound came.

He took another step, paused and listened. He took another step and paused again. He proceeded up the stairs one step at a time.

The rent-a-cop is always the first one to die in the movies. This is it. This is the end of Eddie Waters.

Eddie saw the door to the second floor as if he was watching it on a television screen; it got bigger as he moved closer. He recalled seeing this sort of thing happen before, on *The X-Files* probably. These kinds of storylines never ended well, not for the security guard. *If I was Fox Mulder, I'd at least have a gun right now.*

Eddie stepped out into the light of the hallway and looked both directions. Nothing was out of the ordinary as far as he could tell. He moved down the first hallway, stuck to the wall like a magnet. The building seemed unusually quiet all of a sudden. He desperately tried to recall what the hallway was normally like, as if his life depended on it. He tried to be as quiet as he could, but the sound of his clumsy, black security boots echoed off the cement walls.

At the end of the hallway everything appeared to be normal. *See, nothing is wrong. Just do the same down the other hallway, and get the hell out of here!* He returned to the top of the stairs, looking back over each shoulder the entire way.

He walked down the other hallway at a faster pace without stopping to look into each room, but for some reason, he paused in the doorway of the last room - the room with the ladder to the attic. His eyes focused on the pitch-black darkness beyond the square hole in the ceiling. Somehow, he knew something was up there. He could sense it.

He braced himself against the doorframe. *I think I'm having an anxiety attack.* He gasped, pounding his chest, trying to beat air into his lungs. *Anxiety attack. Anxiety attack. Anxiety attack. There! Something moved!*

Eddie saw a woman's head swing down from the hole in the ceiling. The dangling head looked like a zombie's - pale, white, dirty and almost dead - but her eyes peered straight into Eddie's soul. Then she squealed. And he shrieked. The sounds echoed off of the cold cement walls. And the woman disappeared.

Eddie stumbled backwards and fell into the hallway. His mind raced: *This isn't real. This isn't happening.* Eddie's instincts took over and he ran down the hallway, down the steps and out the door. He didn't stop running until he was at the backdoor to the hospital. His hands trembled as he grasped for his keys in a panic.

Once inside Eddie still didn't feel safe. He ran through the hallways, stopping just short of the lobby in order to catch his breath. His shirt was soaked through to the armpits.

Eva, the receptionist, was at her desk, and he didn't want her to see him in his current state. He considered stepping into the bathroom to towel off, but he wasn't ready to be alone in a confined space again.

Eddie wiped his forehead on his sleeve and took a few deep breaths, desperately trying to slow down his heart rate. Taking one last breath, he went for it; he scampered along the wall to the security desk. He plopped down into his chair and pretended to look through the top drawer for something until he started to feel normal. In an attempt to seem cool, calm and collected - to prove nothing was out of the ordinary - Eddie shouted to Eva from across the room, "It's really hot in the boiler room."

Eddie's voice boomed through the quiet, empty lobby and gave Eva a start. They usually sat in silence at their respective desks. Eva nodded, looking surprised and annoyed, and then turned back at her computer screen.

Likewise, Eddie stared at the computer screen in front of him. The last five minutes were such a blur; he was still unsure of what he saw.

That was not real, he told himself. *That was a figment of your imagination.* He so desired for it all to be hallucination that he wished he could somehow prove that his imagination was responsible for this cruel joke or that he could pinch himself awake in a cold sweat in his own bed. Against his will, the scene replayed in his head, but when the woman's head dropped down through the hole, instead of screaming, she said, "Eddie? Are you okay?"

Her voice grew louder. "Eddie? Eddie!"

Eddie almost fell backwards out of his chair. When he recovered, he saw Bea sitting in front of his desk.

"Eddie?" she said again. "Are you okay?"

"Fine. Are you going out to smoke?"

"I should think so," she said, eyeing him. "Is that alright?"

"Sure. I could use some fresh air."

"Geez, you look like you've seen a ghost."

Eddie smiled. *I think I have.*

Bea's presence helped Eddie calm down. He tried to focus on their conversation, but while Bea talked, his mind wanted to revisit the boiler room. It made him feel schizophrenic and jittery. And he realized, in the midst of everything, he forgot to finish his rounds. The idea of locking all the doors and turning off all the lights by himself was dreadful.

When Bea stopped talking to take a puff of her cigarette, Eddie asked, "How would you like to accompany me on my rounds this evening? I forgot to lock up the kitchen."

Bea's face lit up. "Sure, Eddie. I would love to."

Eddie made sure Bea talked the entire time, leaving no room in the conversation for silences. When they were done, Eddie pushed her into the elevator, pressed her floor number, stepped back and waited for the door to close. "Thanks for coming with me."

"It was my pleasure," Bea said with her usual, gentle smile. "Now I know where to find you if I need you at night."

The elevator door closed, and Eddie thought: *This will be the first test to see if I have another hallucination.* The word "hallucination" echoed in his head. *Hallucination. Hallucination. Hallucination.* It was nine-thirty when he returned to his desk, which meant he only had a half an hour to regain his composure before he'd be forced to leave the lobby and confront the shadows of the parking lot.

On the way home that night, the act of driving kept Eddie's mind busy, at first. He merged into the sparse traffic of the expressway, chose his lane and set his speed. Then, he was left to his thoughts again. The rear view mirror captured his attention. Eddie tried to fight his imagination with reason and logic. *The car is empty*, he argued. *I checked. There is nothing to look for in the mirror.*

But there are some things that can't be achieved with rationale, and before Eddie could contest any further, his eyes were looking deeply into the rearview mirror. He expected something to happen. He stared into it as if it should be a window into the world's deepest and darkest secrets. He saw an endless stretch of road passing away from him. The headlights from a few cars in the distance were shining like tiny, little stars, and he was the object of their gaze. For a brief moment, he saw himself as a deer caught in headlights trying to cross a busy road at night, managing to jump over the guardrail just before the car rushed by, slipping into the darkness never to be seen again.

A car horn blared.

Eddie was drifting into the left lane while the car was trying to pass him. He jerked the wheel to the right to make the correction. The car swerved back and forth before stabilizing in the center of the lane. "My God," Eddie said. His palms started to sweat, making it difficult for him to grip the wheel.

I told you there was nothing in the backseat, he scolded himself. *Just drive home without killing yourself, and forget this whole thing. You're not crazy, and nobody's out to get you.*

Eddie turned on the radio as a distraction, and a radio personality said, "Don't we believe in second chances, Rick? Isn't that part of the American Dream?"

Another person responded, "Not if you're a criminal, Rory. We've been over this. Once you commit a crime, you're not entitled to the American Dream anymore. But we're up against a break here at 'The Rick and Rory Show' on WGRR, *The Rapid, 107.7*. We'll take some of your calls when we return. Stay tuned."

Eddie was more than happy to listen to the radio commercials in a mindless daze as he finished his commute. At his apartment complex, he sat in his car and stared at his building. He imagined eyes peering at him through the floorboards as he ascended the stairs to his dark, possibly empty apartment.

If what happened was real, he thought, *there is no reason I should be afraid of going home. The woman would still be in the boiler room and a long way from my apartment. I shouldn't be afraid to be alone. I should only be afraid of going back into the boiler room. But what if the woman followed me home?* He tried to be reasonable. *If the woman could follow me home, she'd have a car. And if she could afford a car, she wouldn't be in the boiler room at all.*

Eddie exited the car and walked toward the stairwell, but a new thought entered his head that stirred his fears even more. He could not be certain whether the situation was or was not a figment of his imagination. If there was a real person hiding in the attic of the boiler room, he could prove it. However, if it was in his mind - possibly because of some deep-rooted issue with which he struggled in the subconscious regions of his being was coming to light in the form of a mysterious woman - then it was entirely possible that the woman *could* follow him home. And not only follow him home, but follow him wherever he and his imagination went.

Eddie envisioned himself becoming a frantic lunatic obsessed with his imaginary stalker to the point where everyone thought was crazy. He would become a prize-winning project for some greedy team of doctors trying to discover when and why he had gone off the deep end. *I'm out of my mind. I'm too old to be afraid of a monster hiding in the closet. I need to get some rest.*

Eddie raced up the stairs to his apartment with his key in hand, prepared for a quick entry. Once inside his apartment, he turned on all the lights and the television and sat down on the couch with a cold beer. Then it occurred to him, once again, that it was Friday. In his current state of mind, this minor detail grew into a massive, hideous beast staring him straight in the eye and snarling at him. He suddenly wished more than anything that he could prove that the woman was in fact real, and he found it entirely logical that he should return to the boiler room that very evening and confront the inexplicable woman. But there was no way around it; he'd have to spend the entire weekend at his empty apartment, alone.

Six

"Do you know how to play Euchre?" she asked.

"Of course," he said. "We'd need four people for that. Do you know how to play Rummy?"

"Is that the one where you hold all your cards until the end or the one where you put down the books and runs as you go?"

"As you go."

"I like that one. I haven't played that one since I was a kid."

"I'll go first because you dealt," he said. He drew a card from the top of the deck and then discarded the seven of clubs from his hand.

"I pick up a card to start, right?" she asked.

"Yes, but if you pick up the seven of clubs I discarded, you'll have to play it on this turn."

"Yes, I remember now."

They played silently for a few rounds.

"If you could live anywhere," she asked finally, "where would you live?"

"I don't know. I would probably stay in the Midwest, I think. Michigan, maybe. Definitely not Ohio."

"Ha! Why not?"

"Have you been to Ohio?"

"Once when I was a kid, but we just drove through."

"It's just so flat. I don't know. It just feels boring. I might consider Wisconsin or Minnesota."

"Have you ever been there?" she asked.

"No, but I like cheese and beer."

"I bet you were funny as a kid," she said.

"Chubby. That's what you mean. Admit it. You bet I was chubby as a kid."

"No, I meant funny."

"Funny because I was chubby."

"…"

"Boom! There's that ace you were looking for," he said, slamming down a book of aces.

"Maybe I was laughing because I thought you were a chubby kid."

"Yeah, yeah, yeah," he said. "How about you? Where would you go?"

"Canada. I would definitely go to Canada," she said. "And I think these kings and these queens more than make up for your pathetic little aces - emphasis on little, man."

"First, you say you're going to leave America for Canada. Now, you're implying I'm a little man. Outrageous."

"What kind of house would you want?" she asked, ignoring his comment.

"A nice house. Two stories at least. Maybe all wood, you know? I like that log cabin feel."

"Me too," she said. "I was going to say a log cabin. I want a big one - one you can get lost in. I like those ones that have really high ceilings."

"On a nice, big, wooded piece of land?"

"Yes, exactly. By a lake too. And I'd have a boat, and I'd go fishing. By the way, I only have one card left, just so you know."

"I'd like that," he said. "I'd go fishing with you."

"I'd like that, too."

"What kind of car would you drive?" he asked.

"I'd have a slick, black Lexus SUV to pull my boat."

"You've thought about this before, haven't you?"

"Probably too many times. I've had plenty of time to sit and think about it."

"What do you mean?" he asked.

"Nothing," she said. "I'm out!"

"You always win."

"This is the first time we've played Rummy."

"You've won almost all the other games we've played so far."

"Not all of them," she said. "But most. Lose gracefully, would you? And I think I'm entitled to a prize, aren't I?"

He rolled his eyes.

"Don't act like you don't like it."

He gave her a kiss.

"Thank you."

"Your deal," he said.

"You want more of this, do you?"

"You better believe I do," he said, shuffling the cards. "What countries would you travel to?"

"I'd go to Paris, for sure," she said. "No doubt about it."

"Why Paris?"

"Paris just seems so romantic. I've always wanted to go. How about you?"

"Somewhere in Europe. Germany, Switzerland, Italy."

"Italy."

"Or maybe Scotland or Ireland. Anywhere really."

"Me too. I want to get out and see the world."

"Me too."

"I'd like to…" She stopped.

"What?" he asked.

"Nothing."

"You'd like to what?"

She shrugged.

Since everyone was accounted for, Eddie took the opportunity to sneak off to the break room. It was a small room down the hall and around the corner from the lobby. There were a few windows, two round tables accompanied by folding chairs and three vending machines in the break room, and dim lighting made the room seem abandoned.

The first vending machine was a Coke machine from which he bought a beverage every day - either Coke or Sprite. The second vending machine had an assortment of candy bars and small bags of chips, from which he bought some form of chocolate. The third vending machine had a strange mix of canned fruit, cracker snacks and sandwich halves, from which he bought a turkey and cheese sandwich. Eddie sat at the table and ate quickly. Although he was not told one way or the other, he was unsure if he could eat at the security desk.

When he was finished eating, he decided to do the rounds early. He was anxious to deal with the demon, and he was determined not to be distracted by all of his previous fears that passed through his head over the last seventy-two hours. He was going to go straight up to the attic and find out exactly who was up there.

I'm not a pussy, he thought. *Just get it done.*

As Eddie walked out the back door of the hospital and the building came into view, his resolve wavered. *I should walk around the building first. You know, see if there's anything out of order.*

His nerves weakened as he approached each corner, but after making each turn, he found nothing out of the ordinary. *This is ridiculous. It probably didn't even happen*, he thought. *I probably just got myself all worked up from what Brad said about people being in there, and I psyched myself out. I bet that's what happened.*

Eddie turned the final corner and headed for the door. His hands were sweaty and shaking; it was a difficult task to get the door open. Inside, he didn't bother to turn on the lights, for it was early enough that there was enough light coming through the windows to illuminate his way. He lifted his foot up to the first stair, but his feet were heavy and sluggish, as if they were resisting his actions. Holding his breath, he proceeded as quietly as he could and listened for anything unusual. The boiler room was full of unidentifiable, sporadic noises. It would be close to impossible to recognize anything out of the ordinary.

At the top of the stairway, Eddie hesitated. He poked his head around the corner, looked both ways and retreated like a frightened cartoon mouse peeking out of an arched hole in the kitchen wall. There was nothing out of sort, as far as he could tell.

Stepping out into the hallway felt like reaching the summit of an insurmountable mountain. Despite all his natural inclinations, he somehow moved toward the mysterious entrance to the attic. He entered the room with a confidence foreign to him.

The woman does not exist. Eddie was determined, like an atheist denouncing God. And before he could protest, his voice questioned the heavens, "Hello?" His own voice spooked him. He awaited a response. Now that it was out in the open, he couldn't wait for the moment to be over, when he could move on as if nothing ever happened.

Eddie seemed to be watching himself as if he was watching a movie. He watched the security guard challenge an unseen opponent. "I know you're there," he said. "I can hear you breathing. I don't want any trouble. I just want to talk to you."

Now, why in the world would you say that, you crazy security guard? Eddie criticized. *Get the hell out of there.*

The security guard continued, "I just want to help you."

Get the hell out of there! Just go, Eddie begged.

"Who are you?" a woman's voice asked in a whisper. It was almost inaudible.

Instantly, Eddie was back in his body. He stumbled backwards. His vision blurred. "I'm going to pass out," he said. He began to wobble back and forth, and as he reached for the nearest wall, he caught a glimpse of two eyes peering down at him from the hole in the ceiling.

Eddie blacked out, and his body collapsed onto the cold, cement floor.

Seven

"Hello?" he asked. "Marilyn? Are you there?"

"Is that you, Eddie?"

"It's me."

"I thought you were going to come over after work?"

"I know. I'm sorry. I couldn't wait."

"I'm glad you're here."

"I'm glad *you're* here. I was worried something happened to you when you didn't respond."

"I'm sorry. I must have dozed off. Come on in."

Eddie climbed on top of her, kissing her neck.

"Well, hello," she said. "I missed you too."

Eddie kissed a trail up to her jawline and followed it to her chin, then up to her mouth. He took his shirt off.

"Hold on." She stopped.

"What?"

"Do you think we should?"

"Yes."

"I don't know."

"I want to."

"Me too."

They continued to kiss.

She stopped again. "But this is complicated."

"It is."

"How would it ever…"

"We can make it work," he said.

"How?"

"I don't know. Love is always complicated."

"But this is even more complicated."

"Why?"

"It just is. I don't think we should. We can't go any farther. We can't."

Eddie stopped. "You're right."

"But I want to."

"I know. Me too."

"Besides, we don't have any protection."

"No, we don't."

"We can't do it without protection."

"No, we can't."

"We better slow down."

"I know." After a moment, he said, "Marilyn, I think you should move in with me."

"What?"

"I want you to move in with me," he repeated. "I mean, there's no reason for you to live here anymore. You can come stay with me."

"I don't know about that. You're not thinking straight right now."

"Yes, I am. That way I can see you whenever I'm not working. It'll be easier for you too. And nicer. We can get you a job. It's going to be getting cold pretty soon. Wouldn't you rather live in an apartment with heat? Doesn't that sound nice?"

"Yes, it does, but I can't."

"Why not?"

"Don't you think we're moving a little too fast?" she asked.

"Too fast? No, of course not. I mean, I love you, and you love me. Right? What's the difference how fast…"

"I can't. I just can't." She began to cry.

"What's stopping you?"

"What if it doesn't work out?" she said.

"Okay. If things don't work out - but they will - by then you'll have a job, and if you don't want to stay with me anymore, I can help you find your own place."

"It's not that simple. I can't get a job."

"Why not?"

"I just can't. Okay."

Eddie's heart was being ripped in half from top to bottom. She could see the anguish on his face.

"I'll think about it," she said. "Okay? How about that? Can I at least think about it?"

"Of course you can." He wiped the tears from her eyes.

"I'll think about it. Okay?"

"I love you," he said. "Really. I do."

"I love you too."

Exhibit Thirteen: (Di)vision

When Eddie came to, his head was spinning and his vision was blurry. Someone was holding up his head and putting a water bottle to his lips. He envisioned himself at home as a kid, sick, and his mother was taking care of him. One of his older brothers walked into the room and demanded his mother bring him to meet up with his friends. His mother dropped the water bottle and left him. Eddie heard himself say, "Mom. Don't go." His mother reappeared in the doorway and looked at him with a strange, unfamiliar face, and asked, "Who are you?"

Eddie cringed and cowered like a frightened dog. "Who are you?" he replied.

"I'm the woman you found in the attic."

Eddie's vision cleared, and he knew exactly where he was. Sitting before him was a young woman holding an old water bottle up to his mouth. He was repulsed by the mangled and dirty lip. He pushed it away.

"Who are you?" the woman asked again.

Eddie rubbed his eyes clear, and he saw the woman for the first time. She looked young, possibly in her mid-to-late twenties. He couldn't tell for sure. She had blond hair that curled down to her neckline and shined. She had gentle eyes. She was wearing a stained white tank top and thin blue pants. On her feet, she wore a flimsy pair of slippers.

"I work here," he said. "Did I black out?"

"Yes. Only for a couple of minutes."

Eddie took a moment to gather himself. He sat up and leaned against the wall - the one he'd reached for when he collapsed. The room was still spinning.

"Did you hit your head on the way down?" asked the woman, guiding her hand gently through his hair.

"No, I don't think so."

"Are you sure you don't want some water?"

"No. That's okay. Thank you. I probably should get going. I have to finish my rounds." Eddie rose to his feet, and he felt pain in his knees and elbows. His legs wobbled as his feet shuffled across the floor. His eyes seemed to be rolling around in their sockets. The woman jumped up just in time to catch him before he fell again, and she helped him to the ground. Once he was seated again, the woman moved away from him and sat against the adjacent wall.

"What are your rounds?" she asked in a soft voice.

The question reminded Eddie that he couldn't just get up and walk away. The situation was much more complicated. The woman had been living in the boiler room. *I can't just let it go*, he thought. *I'm supposed to do something. It's my job.*

Their eyes connected. The mysterious woman was staring up at him with big, sad eyes that were pleading with him as if to say, *What are you going to do with me?*

The woman, who had helped him only moments ago, now appeared in a new light. Their roles immediately reversed. Her future depended entirely on him. He was in need, and she helped him. Now, she was in need.

Eddie bent slightly, resting his hands on his knees, trying to assume a less imposing posture. He asked, in what he hoped to be a gentle voice, "Who are you?"

The woman cast her eyes to the floor, hiding behind a few strands of hair, and she coiled her legs into her small frame.

"I'm not going to hurt you," Eddie said. "You helped me. I want to help you in return."

"I'm homeless," she whispered. "Yes. I'm homeless."

Although Eddie imagined this very scenario several times since he started at the hospital, he was completely unprepared for it.

"Are you going to call the police?" she asked.

"No." He paused to think, but the throbbing in his head made it difficult. "How long have you been living here?"

"Since I saw you last." The woman lifted her head and raised her eyes to meet his.

"It's alright," Eddie said. "I mean no harm. I'm a security guard, but it's not what you think." He shifted in her gaze. "What is your name?"

She averted her eyes again. The question made her retreat like a turtle into its shell.

"I just want to thank you for being nice to me. You don't have any other place to go?"

She shook her head.

"I won't make you leave. I want to help you. Have you been staying in the attic?"

The girl nodded.

"Do you have any food?"

She did not respond.

"How long has it been since you've eaten?"

"Since before I came here," she said at last.

Eddie did the math. *At least three days, maybe four.* Eddie said, "I will get you something to eat." He stood to leave, feeling more stable with a new sense of determination. "I still don't know what to call you."

"Marilyn," she whispered. "You can call me Marilyn."

"Okay, Marilyn. I'll be back. Make sure you don't come out unless you know it's me."

As Eddie was leaving, he was stopped in his tracks.

"Thank you, sir," Marilyn said.

The words sent goose bumps down his spine.

Eddie checked the time as he rushed through the first floor hallway. He had been gone for almost an hour already. He scampered around locking up doors and turning off lights as he made his way back to the vending machines. By the time he reached the break room, he was out of breath. Everything had happened so fast in the last hour. He didn't realize that he left his wallet at the security desk until he got to the break room. Making his way to the front lobby, he combed his hair with his hands and checked the neatness of his uniform. *How could Eva not be suspicious of my activities?*

Pausing in the hallway, he made one last effort to look normal before he hurried to his desk, grabbed his wallet and headed right back to break room.

Eva was reading as usual and didn't seem to notice.

Eddie rifled through his wallet to find he only had $1.65. What should he buy? He had a crucial decision to make. She had water, but not very much, and if he bought her a bottle of water he wouldn't have much left for food. Candy was the cheapest, but it wasn't nutritious. If he bought a sandwich, he wouldn't have enough left for anything else. He could buy a piece of fruit and a small snack for fifty cents each and a candy bar for sixty-five cents. *That way she could spread out what she ate until tomorrow night,* he thought. *I'll bring her some more water then, too.* He decided to go with an apple, a package of crackers and a Payday.

It was getting late. Eddie needed to get back to the front desk. He ran through the hallway, out the back door, into the boiler room and up the stairs. He hurried to the room with the ladder to the attic, and to his surprise, he found it empty.

This is the end, he thought. *She's never going to appear again and I'll go crazy trying to make people believe this story. They'll call me delusional, psychotic and all the other adjectives that come along with…*

"You're back," Marilyn said, peaking down from the attic.

"I brought you some food," he said.

#

Eddie returned to the lobby feeling unstable; his blood was dancing the jitter bug in his veins. He paced back and forth behind the security desk, unable to be still. The complexities of his new circumstances were staggering. He could barely make any sense of it.

Bea, on time as usual, made her way across the lobby. Timing is often, as they say, everything. In Bea's case, she was almost always in the right spot at the right time. Eddie was pleased to see her.

"I didn't want to have a smoke," she said, "but I had to come down and make sure you're worth the money we're paying you."

"That was mighty nice of you." Eddie tried to match her jovial mood. "I would hate to be burdened with the guilt of getting paid without working."

Eddie wheeled Bea to the patio and parked her next to the flower box. That evening was hot, even warmer than usual.

Bea inspected the flowers with her hand. "My flowers are growing so well, aren't they?"

"They really are." Four or five of the flowers were beginning to bloom with tall colorful petals.

"They are doing much better than last year."

The conversation moved on to Bea's usual topics: Shirley's deteriorating mind; Sam's health and his absent family; Bob's cruel wife; David's tragic life. As Bea talked, Eddie's thoughts kept wandering back to the woman in the boiler room, Marilyn, whose life was also in disarray. And he remembered how, in college, he would fantasize about all the needy people he might help throughout his career and all the fulfillment he hoped to get out of it. *This may be my first chance to make a real difference,* Eddie thought, and for the first time, Marilyn's mere existence electrified him.

THE GRAND RAPIDS TIMES
Suspected Accomplice Arrested
Escape Plot Uncovered

Earlier today, Grand Rapids Police apprehended local resident Edward Waters, twenty-two. Waters is suspected of aiding and abetting Norma Baker, twenty-four, who escaped from the Fifth Street Women's Correctional Facility in June.

Baker confounded law enforcement for weeks before authorities launched a citywide manhunt, which resulted in Baker's capture on Sunday. Baker was discovered in the attic of the boiler room at the Fifth Street Community Hospital by two local detectives, whom authorities have yet to name. At the time of his arrest, Waters was working as part of a security team assigned to the Fifth Street Community Hospital, where he has been employed with North American Security since June.

According to a statement released by the Grand Rapids Police Department, Waters was "brought in for questioning in regards to his relationship with Norma Baker because [Waters'] fingerprints were found at the scene. Further investigation will be necessary in order to determine whether or not Waters' fingerprints were there as a result of work-related activities."

Authorities declined to comment further; however, sources close to the investigation have described Baker's hideout as "well-supplied," indicating she most likely had an accomplice.

A spokesman for North American Security said Waters did not have a criminal record at the time he was hired, and he was cleared for employment using a standard background check.

Charges against Waters have yet to be filed.

Exhibit Fourteen: Intention

We face unexpected crossroads every day, where we have to make choices that can determine the trajectory of our lives. We can choose to be a Good Samaritan or a thief, to follow the law or to break it, to follow our own instincts or to follow the crowd. One good choice may lead to better choices. One undesirable turn may lead to more undesirable options. And it is the mysterious, unknown roads that cause alarm. Those roads are often the hardest to choose. Unknown paths have the potential to be the most thrilling and the most rewarding, but we fear entering forbidden territory, because the consequences are unclear. Therefore, each crossroad we face presents a complicated conundrum.

Eddie was standing at a crossroad. He was sitting in his car outside of the supermarket, watching people come and go as they pleased without a care in the world, and he had a decision to make. He could forget the whole thing and drive away. He would, then, report Marilyn and have her removed from the boiler room. *If I did that,* he thought, *Marilyn would be thrown out of the building, and nobody would give her a second thought, much less a helping hand. How could I live with myself knowing I did that to her?*

Or he could help her. He could buy her some basic necessities: a blanket, a pillow, a sweatshirt, t-shirts, socks and shoes. He could provide her with a basic food supply: bread (carbs), peanut butter (protein), cheese (dairy), crackers (for the cheese), Pop-Tarts, chocolate (by request) and a gallon of drinking water. *That would be helpful,* Eddie thought. *What would be the harm in that?* He couldn't know what the harm would be; he'd never been a homeless woman's benefactor before.

Either way, whichever decision Eddie made, he would not be able to reverse it. He was faced with a problem that was larger than his ability to reason it out, and he had nothing to go on except for his instincts. He had to rely on his moral compass.

It would be wrong, he thought, *for me to deny someone help when they truly need it, especially when I have the means to do so. Right? Do to others as you would have them do to you. Right? I have the opportunity and the means to help this woman. Therefore, I must.*

Eddie stepped out of his car, and slammed the door shut. And, with that, his decision was made.

Eddie worked his way through the supermarket, snaking through the aisles one at a time, tossing items into the cart, regardless of cost. At checkout, his items seemed weird and random, which made him nervous. The feeling reminded him of the incident at the church several weeks earlier. *Screw that,* he thought. *Screw them, and screw that ugly woman. This is America, damn it. I'll do what I want.*

Eddie's confidence dwindled as soon as a barcode on one item failed to scan at the register. The newly-hired cashier needed assistance from the manager in order to use the intercom system to call for a price check. The item in question was, of course, the oddest and most incriminating item he had.

"White, women's tennis shoes," the cashier said into the phone. "Dunlop. Yes, the ones with the stripes. Size seven. Okay, thanks."

Every customer within a twenty-foot radius was now well-informed of Eddie's unusual purchase. Eddie paid his bill in a hurry and scampered out the door.

Free of the supermarket, he felt a renewed conviction in his noble quest. *This is America, for God's sake. I'll by women's shoes if I damn well please.*

When Eddie got back to his apartment, he surveyed his haul, and he saw that it was good. Food, clothes and bedding for a homeless woman: $107.59. The items cost him a large portion of his paycheck, but the satisfaction of helping someone in need was priceless.

As Eddie sat alone in his apartment, he imagined The Volleyball Player becoming Marilyn. He envisioned checking into an expensive hotel in Paris with her. They had sex for the first time in weeks. He was on top. She was quiet. Afterwards, they wandered the streets of Paris, hardly talking.

Eddie was disappointed when he saw the Eiffel Tower. It didn't seem as big or beautiful or romantic as he imagined. While he was looking up at the iconic structure, she tugged on his sleeve and said, "Let's go back to the hotel."

She went to bed. Eddie slipped out the door and went down to the bar for a drink. He drank his wine and thought, *This can't be how it ends. We have the house and the cars and financial stability. We're supposed to be all set. We should be talking about having a kid and splitting our time between work and family and running away on romantic retreats. We're supposed to be the couple that keeps the fire burning. We're supposed to be the kind of parents that teenage kids walk in on having sex. That's our story,* he thought, thumping his pointer finger on the bar for emphasis.

"Is everything okay, buddy?" asked the bartender.

"Yes. Everything will be fine." He watched the final sip splash around in the bottom as he swirled the chalice in his hand. He threw his head back and poured it down his throat, thinking, *This can't be how it ends...*

The next morning, Eddie awoke fully clothed on the couch in a panic. It was one-thirty in the afternoon. He was going to be late. Scrambling, he retrieved a large, black garbage bag from the kitchen and stuffed the blanket, pillow, sweatshirt, shoes and other non-food items into it. He grabbed the bag of food and raced out the door, wearing the same uniform from the previous day. He stuffed the bags into the passenger seat of his car and sped away.

He looked at the clock: one-forty. He slowed to a normal speed. "I'll make it." Weakened by hunger, he gave in and ate three of Marilyn's Pop-Tarts for breakfast.

Eddie arrived at the hospital carrying the bag of food. Brad said, "Someone's hungry today, 'ey?"

"I slept in too long this morning."

"Don't let the people upstairs see you eating on the job," Brad added, on his way out the door. "Have a good day."

The first thing Eddie did, after punching in, was slip into the break room and consume the rest of the Pop-Tarts like a mad man. Then he hid the bag behind a chair in the back corner. On his way out of the break room, he checked to see if the bag was visible from the doorway. *That will have to do*, he thought.

That day, Eddie was distracted. He checked his watch repeatedly. The residents either didn't care or didn't notice. When it was time for dinner, he hurried to the break room to check on his stash. Everything appeared to be as expected, so he could go about his business as usual. He bought a few items out of the vending machine and sat in the break room eating a poor meal of processed food, sugared soda and candy.

At the security desk, Eddie studied the camera feeds to determine how to hide his package when he went out the back door. The camera was aimed straight at the door. As far as he could tell, he just needed to keep the bag centered in front of him, and he would be home free. The stage was set. Everything was in place. It was all going smoothly - almost too smoothly. The apparent lack of danger almost ruined Eddie's excitement.

At seven-thirty, Eddie began the rounds, but he didn't head straight for the boiler room. This time, he started in the basement, locking up the doors and turning out the lights. He finished all the rounds before ending up back at the break room. Eddie picked up the stash and headed toward the back door. Pausing below the camera, he positioned the bag directly in front of his torso, trying to maintain a natural posture. He took a deep breath and went for it, walking fast until he was out the door and past the camera's view. The bag rustled in his unsteady hands. The excitement was back.

Eddie rushed out to the boiler room, key in hand. It was strange to desire going *into* the boiler room, but lots of his fears had changed recently. Once inside, he turned on the lights and stopped to listen. Nothing seemed out of place. The building seemed so abandoned that he began to wonder if Marilyn had gotten scared and left on her own.

Eddie took one step at a time, trying to be as quiet as possible, cautiously entering the last room. As he approached the ladder, he looked up into the dark hole. He didn't see or hear anything moving. He kicked the wall twice, but the sound wasn't as loud as he had hoped. "Hello?" he whispered.

"I'm here," she responded immediately. Her head appeared in the opening. She had been hiding so close to Eddie that when she moved it made him jump. "Sorry," she said. "I didn't mean to scare you."

"I brought you some..." Before he finished his sentence, she jumped down, tore the bag out of his hands and rummaged through it.

"Thank you so much," she said. Her head was almost entirely inside the bag. "I'm so hungry."

"You're welcome. I brought you some water and some other things too, but I can't just bring them out to you. We'll have to figure out a system." Eddie couldn't tell if Marilyn was listening as she ate. "I'm going to run down to the boiler room and finish up a few things. I'll be right back."

"Thank you, thank you, thank you," she said as he left the room.

On his way back from the basement, he noticed that the lock on the boiler room door consisted of a simple bolt construction and was equipped with a knob that would allow someone to lock and unlock the door from the inside. This minor detail could be the solution to their problem. He tested it by locking and unlocking it two or three times before he was fully satisfied that it would work.

He returned to the room at the end of the hallway and found her sitting on the floor dipping a cracker in peanut butter. He sat down on the floor, leaned up against the opposite wall and watched her eat.

In his previous encounter his nerves had been rattled, which hindered his ability to be observant. Now, he noticed that her toenails, however dirty, had been trimmed recently. They were shaped neatly, although they were beginning to get long. They had been painted at some point, with a bright red polish that was almost entirely chipped off.

How does a homeless girl get nail polish? he wondered.

She sat with her legs tucked under her to the side, and her dark blue pants were pulled tight to her thighs.

He noticed she had a nice figure. Through her stained tank top, he could see the outline of her bra, which alone prevented her from being exposed. Also, he noticed her big eyes were a stunning blue and were highlighted by strong cheekbones and full maroon lips. In other circumstances, groomed and with proper attire, she could easily be the belle of the ball. He averted his eyes lest she caught him staring.

Eventually, when her monstrous appetite was beginning to subside, they agreed upon a plan for him to drop off the other supplies later that evening, and he departed.

GRlive.com
'Waters often disappeared,' Co-Workers Say

According to a source at the Fifth Street Community Hospital, Waters often disappeared for long periods of time while he was on the job. Part of Waters' duties included evening rounds - turning off lights, locking doors and checking various rooms. The same source confirmed that most security guards would take a half an hour to complete the tasks, but some nights, Waters would be gone for an hour or more.

Waters was often absent-minded on the job as well. Another North American Security guard, who was also assigned to the Fifth Street Community Hospital, said Waters repeatedly daydreamed on the job while he was supposed to be supervising residents. According to the source, who wished to remain anonymous, Waters often seemed preoccupied with his thoughts.

Waters' job performance has raised several questions. Security footage released by the hospital shows Waters behaving suspiciously near the exit that leads to the boiler room where Norma Baker was found. In one instance, Waters appears to be concealing a large bag. Other instances show Waters behaving erratically, running in and out of the door multiple times.

Administrators at the Fifth Street Community Hospital are now under investigation as well. A recent incident involved an attempted escape by two residents that lead to the death of one. No reports were filed. Now, an investigation is under way to determine whether the administrators responded according to protocol. Waters' involvement is unclear.

Exhibit Fifteen: Confrontation

As Eddie entered the front door of the Fifth Street Community Hospital he whistled a happy tune, and he was unaware of doing so. He was preoccupied. Over the weekend, Eddie and Marilyn had taken their relationship to the next level at last. In twenty-two years of life, Eddie had imagined countless scenarios in which he'd lost his virginity, none of which came close to the real experience. Marilyn's naked body was hairier than he'd expected. As he nestled in between her legs, her leg hair scratched his thighs, and her bush - thick with tangled, matted, greasy pubic hair - poked at his midsection. Her body smelled like cheese, and her skin was rough, like sand paper. And Eddie had a difficult time getting the condom on; he should have practiced first. To make an awkward situation worse, getting inside her was a challenge. In the movies, people make seamless transitions from foreplay to fornication. Marilyn had to readjust under him several times to make it work. By the time their bodies were unified, Eddie climaxed with little satisfaction. In all of his daydreams about that moment, he never imagined there would be so much fluid to be cleaned up. The blanket Eddie bought for Marilyn had to be replaced. The only thing that kept Eddie from being embarrassed was the discovery that Marilyn too had been a virgin. Nevertheless, his outlook on life was transformed. He was in love, and he couldn't help but let it show.

"Why are you so happy today?" asked Brad, who was sitting at the security desk.

"No reason."

"At ease, soldier." Brad motioned for Eddie to take a seat.

Eddie sat down. "What's going on?"

"I hate to be the bearer of bad news on your happy day, but somebody has to do it." Brad leaned in close, as far as the desk would allow, lowered his voice and said, "Bea passed away over the weekend."

Eddie's jaw dropped. When he managed to get a sound out of his mouth, the noise was more like a hiccup than an audible word.

"I know," Brad said. "It was so unexpected. A nurse aide found her Sunday morning. Heart failure, I think. But I'm not sure. They're still looking into it. Rumor has it that Bea reported chest pains to a nurse aide the night before, but they overlooked it. Some members of Bea's family are getting involved, looking to press charges. Negligence, I guess. To tell you the truth, I wouldn't put it past them. I mean, we have some bad staff here during the day, and third shift is terrible, but it's the worst on the weekend. It was bound to lead to something like this. I just wish it didn't have to come down on Bea like that. If they asked me, I'd testify against them."

"That's awful." At that moment, he was feeling extra emotional anyway - being in love. He couldn't help but tear up, and he turned away from Brad to try to hide it.

"Just be careful out there today," Brad said, motioning toward the residents outside. "It's a touchy subject for some of them." Brad picked up his bag and left the building without saying goodbye to the residents.

Eddie scanned the security log to orient himself to the day's comings and goings. It was not going to be a normal day. Sure enough, Sam, Bob, Shirley and David were all checked out - everyone except Bea. Eddie swallowed hard, trying to gulp down his emotions before he went outside.

David and Shirley were in their usual spots. There was enough room in between them for Bea's wheelchair. They either did it out of habit or out of respect. Either way, the sight made his stomach turn.

"Good afternoon, David. How are you today?" Eddie tried to sound steady.

"I'm good…How are…you, Eddie?"

"I'm fine. You know. Hanging in there."

David didn't waste any time. "Did you…hear…about Bea?"

"Yeah, I did."

"Bob says…they just…let her…die up there," David continued. "They didn't…care…that she was…dying."

Eddie nodded. He turned to Shirley. "How are you?"

Shirley was lost in a daze, and she was startled to hear the sound of her own name. She looked around, confused.

"How are you today?" Eddie repeated.

"Oh, hello, Eddie. I didn't see you there." Shirley didn't answer the question; instead, she took a puff from a half-smoked cigarette. A line of ash fell from the end of it and dispersed as it hit the ground. "Didn't you quit?"

"No. I had the weekend off, like usual."

"Oh," Shirley said, and then returned to her daze.

Eddie could see Sam and Bob sitting out on the patio. Bob was struggling to light a cigarette that was hanging from Sam's mouth. They had been spending more and more time on the patio lately. The conversation on the patio was going something like this:

"They don't care about us, Sam. If we're not careful, we're going to be next," Bob said. "The next time you're having heart problems, you think they're going to help you? Not a chance!" Bob pounded his good fist on the armrest of his chair.

"You think so?" Sam was concerned, but he lacked Bob's enthusiasm.

"They want us to die. The government wants you dead, Sam."

"Well now, I don't know about that."

"You think they like helping you pay to live here? You think they like helping you pay for those pills?" Bob waited for a response, then added, "Hell no they don't!"

Sam coughed twice, and a puff of smoke escaped out of his mouth each time. "I know that's true."

"Damn right it's true. We need to get out of here as soon as possible. You need to get out of here more than I do. The government wants you dead. It's only my wife who wants me dead, although she probably already paid off the same nurse that snuffed Bea. I'm probably next. We better get this thing under way." Sam's enthusiasm remained unchanged. Bob continued, "If we can sneak down around the building sometime when the guard isn't looking, we can slip down Franklin Street to Fourth Street. There's a hotel there. I've saved enough money. We can stay there a day or two until things wind down. Then we can go on from there. How are you doing on meds? You got enough?"

"About three weeks' worth."

"Good."

"But where are we going to go after we get to the hotel?"

"We'll go to my house and demand some money from that conniving wife of mine, then we'll head for Detroit and shack up with your family for a while."

Sam nodded, neither agreeing nor disagreeing with the plan.

"Good," Bob said. "It's settled then. We'll leave as soon as we can, probably after the higher-ups go home. So, be ready."

"Sure, Bob," Sam said. "I'll be ready."

On the sidewalk, Shirley asked Eddie, "Did I ever tell you about the time my Momma swore?" Her head, now turned toward Eddie, was shaking on top of her weak, elderly neck.

"How's that?" Eddie leaned up against the building, pretending to be interested, and prepared to recite the story in his head as she went along.

"My daddy was tough, but he was fair. Me and my sisters were a handful. One day my momma was trying to kill one of the chickens, but it just wouldn't set still."

As she spoke, Bob went by, eyeing Eddie suspiciously. He hurried past Shirley and David and went into the building. Eddie caught a glimpse of Bob looking back at him before the electric door closed.

That was odd, Eddie thought.

"'Now you girls quit fooling around,'" Shirley continued. "Go help your momma with that chicken,' Daddy says."

A moment later, Bob returned. He had a backpack hanging off the back of his chair.

That too is strange. "Hey, Bob, are you going hitchhiking today?" asked Eddie.

"No. Why?"

Eddie, caught off guard by his seriousness, back-peddled. "No reason. I just saw you were carrying a backpack today."

"No. I'm not going anywhere." Bob scooted on down the sidewalk.

#

The high Eddie had from being in love mixed with the news about Bea's death made for a nearly unbearable cocktail of emotions. He needed some time alone to think. He was unsure how he'd feel when he went to see Marilyn. He would either be overwhelmed with a renewed excitement to see her, or he would breakdown entirely in her presence. Neither scenario was desirable.

When the residents were taken upstairs for dinner, Eddie retreated to the break room. In all his time working at the nursing home he never encountered anyone else in the there, and he often claimed it as his own private getaway. Occasionally, he would take a copy of *The Grand Rapids Times* from the front desk to read while he ate. If he was careful and folded it neatly, Eva wouldn't make him pay for it when he returned it to the front desk. The paper cost a dollar, and having an extra dollar in his pocket usually determined whether or not he would borrow one. That day just so happened to be one of those days.

It might be good to think about something else for a change, Eddie thought. On his way to the break room, he picked up a paper and said to Eva, "I'm just going to borrow it."

In the break room, Eddie tossed the paper in the direction of the round table at which he was accustomed to sitting. The paper made a clapping nose as it hit the hard surface, slid off of the table and landed in a sloppy mess on the floor. Eddie, as if tossing clothes around in his own bedroom, saw no need - not after finding out about Bea's death - to collect the pile and place it back on the table in a respectable manner. He proceeded with his dinner order: one turkey and cheese sandwich cut into halves and tightly sealed into a triangle of plastic; one fruit cup, representing the healthy part of his diet; one can of cola; and two candy bars, Snickers and Payday. He would need extra comfort food.

Eddie, caught up in his daily routine, forgot about the paper lying in a wreck on the floor until he was nearly finished with his meal. Leaning under the table and collecting the entire pile in one hand without setting down his Payday bar, he thought, *I guess I'm keeping this one*. He flopped the wrinkled wad of papers onto the table.

Eddie shuffled through the papers, stopping to read a headline here or there. Eventually getting annoyed, he made a half-assed attempt to reorganize it, holding the Payday in his mouth to use both hands. When he finished, he held the front page out in front of him and read the main headline:

Escapee Baffles Local Police
Authorities Fumble Investigation

Eddie could only see the top inch of the picture on the front page; the rest was folded under. He held the paper high to let the bottom half fall open, and he gasped, choking on the Payday.

The escapee. The picture. It's Marilyn!

Eddie braced himself against the table. The world seemed to be spinning as if he was the axis. *Oh, my God. Oh, my God. This isn't happening. It couldn't possibly...*

Eddie sat down, took a deep breath and tried to sort out his thoughts. *That's not her,* he thought. *It can't be her. It's just a coincidence.*

Check the picture again to make sure it's...

I can't. I don't want to know.

You have to. At least check for the name. What's the girl's name?

I don't want to know. This can't be happening.

It can't be her. Check the picture and the name, so you can debunk the idea for good.

Eddie picked up the paper slowly as if he could will the picture to change in the process. He looked at the picture again - the eyes, the hair, the lips. He was hoping for something to emerge, something that would prove that the girl was someone else, something that would confirm that it wasn't Marilyn - his first lover. Something was off about the picture, but he couldn't quite explain it. The girl looked very similar to Marilyn, but not nearly as attractive.

"It's not her," Eddie said aloud. He examined the photo once again. "But the resemblance is uncanny." His hands shook, releasing the tension. "What a coincidence."

Eddie, chuckling now, said, "Keep it together, Eddie." He began to read the article: In a statement to the press, Grand Rapids Police confirmed that Norma Baker, twenty-four, escaped from the Fifth Street Women's Correctional Facility (WCF) in downtown Grand Rapids. Baker escaped several weeks ago through a tunnel found in the prison's pantry while she was on a work assignment...

Eddie stopped reading to process the information. *Norma Baker?* he thought. *Marilyn is not Norma. And twenty-four? Marilyn is not twenty-four.* He didn't know how old Marilyn was. At times, she looked way older than him, and at other times, she looked far younger.

Eddie continued reading: Baker was convicted of murdering her stepfather, Gene Mortenson, in Jigsaw, Michigan, in 2000. Mortenson was a well-respected attorney, and the community was deeply saddened by the loss. Throughout the trial, Baker maintained that she acted in self-defense, suggesting Mortenson was sexually abusive. She served seven years at WCF before escaping in mid-June...

"Oh, shit." Eddie jumped out of his chair. "It's her. Oh, my God. It's her!" He grabbed the paper, fled from the room and marched down the hallway.

As he passed the elevator, the bell rang. The doors opened, and Bob and Sam came out into the hallway. Eddie walked passed them without noticing.

He rushed out to the boiler room and up to the attic, only stopping for a moment to recover his breath before calling, "Marilyn?"

After what seemed to be the longest and most nerve-wracking moment of his life, Eddie heard movement. To his surprise, being reassured of her presence made things worse. A small part of him hoped, if she really was this Norma person, that she would be gone, would have disappeared.

"Eddie?" Marilyn whispered from inside the dark attic. "Is that you?"

"Yes, *Norma*, it's me." The name felt strange on his tongue.

Her breathing stopped for a moment, and that was all the evidence he needed to prove that the story in the paper was about her. Her head lowered upside down from the hole in the ceiling just like the first time Eddie saw her. "What did you say?" she asked.

Eddie handed her the paper. She took it and swung herself back up into the attic. He could hear the flashlight click as she turned it on. Then silence filled the room.

She didn't say anything. She climbed down the ladder the way someone would if they were surrendering. When she rested her feet on the floor, she still said nothing. She turned her eyes to Eddie - the same big, beautiful eyes that he saw when they first met. It was all he could do to avoid melting right then and there.

"Is it true?"

She nodded.

Eddie had nothing to say. He felt woozy again. It was all too reminiscent of when he first discovered her, whoever she was. He sat down and felt the cold cement against his legs. It was all too much.

Eddie, too, surrendered. *Why fight it now? It's over. I should have known*, he thought. *I should have been able to put it all together - her strange defensiveness, her refusal to leave this place. How the hell did I miss it?*

"You lied to me," Eddie said at last. "About lots of stuff." It seemed so trivial to say, but in that moment, everything seemed trivial, even the truth.

"Yes, I did."

"Your name is really Norma?"

"Yes."

"Marilyn is much better," he conceded.

"I know," she said.

"How much did you lie about?"

"Just a few minor details."

"Like your name?"

"And being homeless."

"You mean, being a fugitive?"

"But that's it, I swear," she said. "I *swear*. That's it."

"And the murder?" he added. "The paper said you murdered your father."

"Step-father. It was self-defense. I swear. If I couldn't convince a single juror or a single person from that goddamn town, I couldn't expect to convince you."

They stood silent and motionless for a long time. Then, she said with a sense of urgency, "I just want you to know, I need you to know, that whatever happens from here, I really, *truly*, loved you. I *still* love you."

Eddie raised his eyes to meet hers.

"Please know that."

"I love..." Eddie began, but was interrupted by sharp noises coming from the street. Tires screeched. A car honked. Voices yelled angrily. There was more honking. The noises were coming from just outside the boiler room.

Eddie jumped down from the attic and rushed to the nearest window facing the commotion. Trees blocked the view. It was impossible for him to see. The yelling continued, and Eddie recognized the voice. "That's Sam," he said.

Sam was yelling, "Bob! Bob!" His voice was frantic.

Eddie turned and ran down the hallway, down the stairs and out the door. He ran through the trees in the direction of the sound. Branches scraped across his clothing. He guarded his face with his arms.

Sam's voice was getting closer, more desperate. "Bob! Bob!"

Eddie broke through the trees and ran out into the street.

Sam was across the road, pulling at a wheel with his good arm. He was stuck in the grass. His wheels were sinking deeper and deeper as he struggled. He turned his body as far as he could, trying to see Bob behind him, who was idle in the middle of the street.

Bob was slumped over, arms limp at his sides. His chair was rolling slowly down the center of the road, uncontrolled.

Eddie ran and ran and ran and ran. It seemed like a marathon distance from the sidewalk to Bob. He grabbed Bob's chair by the handles, spun him around and ran back the way he came to the hospital, running as fast as he could - sprinting. His black shoes echoed in his ears - *click-clack, click-clack, click-clack* - as he raced up the pavement.

Eddie pushed Bob up the sidewalk as fast as he could. He dashed around the corner, through the parking lot and toward the front door. He gave all he had at the finish, knowing Bob could already be dead. *And it could be my fault!* he thought.

The electric doors didn't open fast enough. Eddie struggled to slow down before Bob's wheelchair crashed into the glass. Bob jolted forward, almost falling out of the chair. The doors finally open. He rushed in. It was all a blur.

"Eva, get the doctor down here. Bob's having a heart attack."

"Take him up on the elevator," Eva commanded. "I'll let them know you're coming." She seemed like she knew what to do, and Eddie was relieved.

Eddie pressed the up button, watching the lighted numbers fall.

Three...

Two...

One…

The door opened, and there was - *thank God* - a doctor in the elevator. Eddie pushed Bob in and explained what happened to the doctor in a breathless panic. The door closed, and the three of them went up together. The doctor checked Bob's neck and chest. All Eddie could do was watch.

By the time the doors opened on the sixth floor, everything was different. There was no hurry, no panic, no going through emergency procedures. There was nothing left to do because it was all over. Bob was dead. His bald, freckled head rested against his chest, limp.

There was no way to tell for sure, according to the doctor, but his preliminary conclusion was heart failure. "Of course," the doctor told Eddie, "we will investigate and find out exactly what happened." The doctor thanked Eddie for his help and said all the usual things a doctor is supposed to say:

"There was nothing else you could have done."

"We did the best we could."

"You did the best you could."

"Bob didn't feel any pain."

"Bob is in a better place now."

Eddie wanted to scream at the doctor, *That's all bullshit! That doesn't mean a goddamned thing. Bob's dead. That's real. That's all that's real about it.*

The doctor dismissed Eddie with a wave of his hand, and a nurse wheeled Bob away, parting a host of onlookers.

Eddie wanted to scream at the crowd, *What the hell are you all looking at? This man is dead. What the hell do you expect to see here?*

The elevator opened again, and Eddie stepped inside. On his way back down to the first floor, he thought, *It was my fault. I should have been there. I was gone. That is why they tried to get away.* The doctor's words ran through his head: *We will investigate. We will find out exactly what happened.*

Eddie realized he left Sam out in the street. The elevator door opened slowly and carelessly. He was running again - down the hallway and out the back door. There was that sound again: *click-clack, click-clack, click-clack.* He ran through the trees and out the other side. Sam was still in the same spot, but he was no longer struggling. He was simply waiting.

Eddie jerked the wheelchair up out of the mud. "I'm sorry," he said, pulling his chair onto the sidewalk and kicking the dirt off of Sam's wheels.

"Where's Bob?" Sam demanded.

"He's on the sixth floor." Eddie pushed Sam across the street.

"Is he okay?"

"I don't know." *Lies.* "Hopefully. The doctors are taking care of him now." *LIES!* He was the doctor now, avoiding the real answer to a simple question about life and death.

He didn't ask what Sam and Bob were doing out there. He knew.

Eddie ushered Sam into the building and watched him get on the elevator. That morning, everything was so simple. He enjoyed his job and he was in love. Now, his whole life had been turned upside down. Bea and Bob were dead, and Marilyn was a convict. It was too much to handle, and he couldn't foresee an end to all the guilt-provoking, finger-pointing questions. The only thing left to do was to go back to his desk and wait for the questions. Where were you? Why were you in the boiler room? Why were you doing the rounds so early?

Why weren't you watching the residents? Where did you find Bob? How did you find him there? What happened? What happened next? And what happened next? And what *fucking* happened *next*? He waited absent-mindedly for the phone to ring or the elevator to open to bring on all the accusations.

Nearly an hour later, Eva came walking toward his desk. She walked with her head down, not making eye contact.

Here it is, Eddie thought. *Here it comes. They sent Eva. Poor Eva. They sent her to do their dirty work, to ask all those mean questions.*

Eva stopped in front of the security desk and waited for Eddie to make eye contact. "Eddie, are you okay?"

That's all? Are you okay? That's it!

"I'm okay." Eddie's voice cracked. "I'm just a little shook up. That's all."

"It's not your fault, alright?" Eva's voice was soft and comforting. "These things happen."

Eddie nodded.

Eva didn't have to say more. They both knew she was just trying to offer something she didn't possess - reassurance. She turned and went back to her desk. That evening ended, and the highly anticipated questions never came. Eddie punched out, waved goodbye to Eva, and left.

#

Eddie was driving in a thoughtless daze, slowly inching along five miles an hour under the speed limit. He tried to leave what happened at work behind him, but the images, the screams and the adrenaline-induced running and panicking all remained in his mind, body and soul.

Bob! Bob! Eddie envisioned him slumped over in his chair. *I ran as fast as I could. What a sad way to die!*

Eddie turned on the radio, hoping to free himself from his thoughts. He turned it up as loud as it could go, so it would be hard for him to think. The first station was playing a song that was too happy; it would be disrespectful to listen to a happy song so soon. The second station was playing a song that was too sad and depressing; it would only intensify the problem. The third station was a sports radio show.

Sports are good. Sports are perfect, Eddie thought. The two radio personalities were making predictions about the upcoming football season. Eddie slipped into a nice, sports-induced coma, somewhat forgetting about his problems.

The radio host switched gears. "I apologize, but we do have to take a quick break." He paused for emphasis. "But we have to talk about this real quick. I'm sure you've heard about this by now. Local authorities are searching for the young woman who escaped from jail.

"According to police, she escaped several weeks ago, but they didn't alert the public or the media until now. Apparently, they were hoping to find her before they had to fess up, like a kid hoping to replace a broken vase before mom finds out. I'm glad our safety is in such capable hands. Anyway, the woman in question is mid-twenties, average height and weight, and she has dirty blonde hair. That is the description given out by the authorities."

His co-host laughed. "I don't know about you, but about half of the young women in the city fit that description."

They both laughed.

"Forget the description, just look for the woman in the orange jump suit."

They laughed again.

"Alright, alright. Our producer is waving at us to move on. So, local authorities are requesting your help to find this Norma Baker. If you have any information please call…"

"Marilyn!" Eddie slammed on the brakes.

Horns honked. Tires squealed. Cars swerved.

Eddie had to jam the accelerator to the floor to avoid causing an accident. He got off at the next exit, drove over the overpass and got back on the expressway going the other way. This time he was driving as fast as traffic would allow, honking, tailgating, swerving and passing any car that got in his way.

Eddie parked his car around the corner from the boiler room. He was running again. *Click-clack, click-clack, click-clack.* He snaked his way through the broken window, disregarding any concern for stealth. There was no need to turn on the lights; he knew his way through the building. On the top floor, he felt along the wall until he found the ladder, and he climbed half way up. "Marilyn?" he called into the darkness. "Marilyn? Are you there?"

"Eddie? What are you doing?" She clicked the flashlight on and shined it in Eddie's eyes.

Eddie shielded his face from the light as he found his way to her bedding.

"What are you doing here?"

"We should talk. Shouldn't we?"

She kept a safe distance, unsure whether or not to be affectionate.

Eddie collapsed onto her bed, exhausted. "I don't know what to do."

"Eddie, what happened?"

"Bob."

"What happened? Is he okay?"

"No. He's not. He's dead. He was probably dead when I got there. I don't know."

She moved closer and nestled against him.

Eddie sighed. "This has been the worst day."

"I know," she said. "I know."

"Bea died Saturday night, too."

"What?"

"That's why Bob and Sam were upset. I just found out about it this morning. They were trying to escape. They couldn't take it anymore."

"Eddie, I don't know what to say."

"There's nothing you can say. That's what happened. Those are the facts."

They embraced in silence.

"Is it true?" Eddie asked, finally. "Is it true that it was self-defense?"

"That's true," she said. "A fact."

"It's true that I love you."

"It's true that I love you too, Eddie."

"Are you mad?"

"No, I'm not mad. I'm a little confused, a lot surprised, some worried and some horrified. I understand why you didn't want to move in with me."

She said nothing.

"How did you, you know, get out?"

"It's a long story."

"I have time. All the time in the world."

"I was in the kitchen for work detail where the supervision is not so good. Only the most trustworthy inmates are allowed to be on kitchen detail. There was a window in the stockroom, way in the back behind all the big cans of food and boxes of paper products. I found it one day when I was stocking the pantry. It didn't have bars on it. I don't think anyone knew about it.

"The place wasn't designed for a jail, you know. Someone must have overlooked the window a long time ago. It opened off the back of the building, and there aren't any fences off the back. Since I was in charge of stocking, which was done in the evenings, it would be easy to sneak away. One day, on my birthday actually, I decided to try to make a run for it. I couldn't live that way anymore."

"That was it. You didn't even have a plan or anything?"

"No. I could see this building from my cell. I had been watching it for years. I knew the patterns of the guards, when they came out here and what they did. I knew I could find a place to hide if I could only get in here. I even noticed you when you first got hired."

"You did not."

"I did."

"How much time did you have left on your sentence?"

"Thirteen years. Once I found that window, I couldn't bear the thought of serving another thirteen years." She looked up at Eddie with her big, sad eyes.

"What's your plan now? Everyone's looking for you."

"I don't know." She grabbed his hand and held it. "Eddie, I didn't mean for this to happen. I promise. I wasn't using you. At first I was, but only because I had no other choice. Then things got out of control. I lied about my name and being homeless, but everything else is true. I didn't intend to meet you, and I didn't intend to fall in love with you. I couldn't help it, I just did."

Eddie hugged her tight. Together, in the dark silence of the boiler room, they cried.

"Everyone's looking for you," Eddie said again.

"I know," she whispered in between muffled sobs. "It's not my fault. I didn't ask for this."

"Shhh. I know."

"He was touching me, and nobody would have believed me. I was trapped."

"Shhh."

She cried and cried until she couldn't cry anymore.

Finally, Eddie sat up. "Let's do it. Let's run away. Let's go to Canada or something."

"What are you talking about?"

"Let's go to Canada. Me and you. Let's just go. We'll see what happens."

"We can't do that. What about you? What about your job?"

"Forget my job. I think I'm going to get fired after this all gets sorted out anyway."

"What?"

"Bob's death tonight. I'm pretty sure it was my fault. They might even be able to press charges for negligence or something. I don't know. I got to get out of here."

"What about your future? What if they catch us? Then you'd go to jail too." She took Eddie's face in her hands and looked him right in the eyes. "Eddie, it wouldn't work. We'd definitely get caught. I love you, but I can't get you involved in this mess."

"I'm already involved."

She shook his face with her hands. "Listen to me. I won't go. I won't do that to you."

Eddie spoke slow and deliberate. "What else are we supposed to do? I can't just let you go."

She kissed Eddie on the lips, his head still in her hands. "Eddie, listen to me. Go home. Get some rest until you start thinking clearly again. You've had a bad day."

Eddie slumped back down onto the bed.

"Tomorrow, you'll think clearly."

"Alright," Eddie said, giving in. He was too exhausted to run any more that night.

THE GRAND RAPIDS TIMES
Waters Charged with Aiding and Abetting

The District Attorney's office has filed aiding and abetting charges against Edward Waters today for harboring Norma Baker, who escaped from the Women's Correctional Facility in June.

According to the Grand Rapids Police Department, Waters was brought in for questioning based on fingerprint evidence found at Baker's hideout. During the initial questioning, Waters admitted that he provided Baker with food, clothing and other supplies, but he denied knowing she was a wanted felon while he was aiding her, authorities said.

Baker was convicted of murder in a highly publicized trial seven years ago. Sources close to the situation confirmed Waters denied knowing anything about her trial.

Baker was using an alias. Waters claimed he learned of her real identity after he saw her picture in the *Times*.

Waters has been cooperative throughout the investigation, said an anonymous officer. When contacted for comment, Waters' court-appointed attorney declined.

Preliminary hearings are expected to begin next week. If convicted, Waters could face up to seven years in prison according to Michigan law.

Exhibit Sixteen: Preparation

The heart wants what it wants. The truth of that statement can be found in the heart of any young man who has ever been caught in the spell of a beautiful young lady; a *goddess*, if you will. Oh, Cecilia! Many men have gone blindly - perhaps courageously, but willingly - into dangerous circumstances in order to pursue their goddess. Oh, Marilyn! And, as history tells us, when the hearts of young men desire something forbidden or condemned, that desire only grows stronger, and the lengths to which they are willing to go in order to oppose the powers that be have proven staggering. In those circumstances, some men succeed, but there are others - we must admit - that fail. The stories of those who succeed are passed on and remembered, and they give strength to those who might try to follow in their footsteps. But the stories of those who fail rarely survive.

With this context in mind, I urge you to try to understand why Eddie was considering going down an ill-advised path, regardless of the obvious, life-changing consequences that would be almost inevitable.

#

The following Friday night, four days after Bob's death, Eddie was lying in his bed staring at the cold, gray ceiling above him. The moonlight from the window harshly cut across the room in elongated stripes, and he wondered if she saw the same light. It was killing him not to know for sure.

Why can't we run? Eddie thought for the millionth time that week. *She has to run. We can't honestly go on like this.*

The thought made Eddie feel more lonely and more sad than anything ever had before. The thought of being without the person he loved indefinitely. His mind was made up. There was only one option.

We must run, he thought. *We must. What else can we do?*

Eddie saw himself running away with Marilyn, Norma, whoever. They would run to Canada and find a little town to hide away. Somehow they would get by. He would become a journalist maybe, or write a book. He always wanted to write a book. If he worked hard enough, maybe she wouldn't have to work. If he worked hard enough, they would make it. They would be happy. It must be possible. He must at least try. He would hate himself forever if he didn't try. He wouldn't be able to live with himself.

Tomorrow, I plan. Tomorrow night, we leave. We must.

#

Eddie was up early the next morning, pacing back and forth, brainstorming. He only had a mere eight hours to get ready before he needed to go get her and set out for Canada. He didn't have a plan yet, and he knew nothing of the details. He didn't even know if she would agree to go with him. They had argued about it all week. But she must; they must go. It would be better than staying here and doing nothing. It would be doing *something*. Nothing would be surrender.

Eddie showered hastily, barely paying any attention to drying off his body. He stood in the center of his room, wearing nothing but a towel, dripping water onto the floor and staring at the mess in his room. His bedding was strewn about, partly on the bed and partly on the floor; clothes were everywhere. An entire garbage bag's worth of trash was sprinkled over it all.

How am going to outrun the law if I can't even work out a laundry system? Eddie criticized himself. He grabbed a mound of clothing and carried it out the door, dropping a trail of unmentionables behind him as he went. In the hallway, in just a towel, he ran down to the laundry room, crammed his clothes in the washer, and slammed the lid shut. Then he rushed back to his apartment collecting the lost items on his way. Everything was happening in a whirlwind now. Eddie hurried to get dressed in dirty, wrinkled clothes. His mind was racing two or three steps ahead of him; his body was struggling to keep up.

Eddie was a bad driver when he was in a hurry, but somehow he made it to the bank safely. He pulled into the drive-through ATM and made cash advances on both of his credit cards. The amount totaled $700, which he hoped would be enough, for now. It would be tight; expenditures were unknown.

Eddie crammed the cash into his wallet, and the money made him feel wired, like he'd committed a crime just by having it in his possession. He took a deep breath and tried to calm himself down. *Okay, okay, what's next?* he thought. *What's next? What's next? The car? The car. Get the car ready.*

He got the oil changed and the gas tank filled. He went through the car wash. *Clean cars are more likely to sneak past customs, right?* He felt better as things were getting done.

At the supermarket, he filled a cart full of food for at least two days. There was no reason to worry about looking suspicious; his pile of food looked similar to everyone else's. And for the first time, Eddie started to really notice individual items and the packaging, and it all seemed odd, worthless actually. All the plastics and cardboards and graphics - nothing seemed edible. And all the people - people counting the calories on every box, and people with calculators and coupons counting every penny, and peopled dressed up, and people in pajamas. The sight saddened him. *What's the point?* he thought. *Honestly, what's the point of all this?* He had a strange sense of purpose and determination. He pushed his cart around the people and products with a renewed fortitude. His escape plan now seemed so logical; he could hardly believe he didn't think of it sooner.

Hair dye, he thought. *She will need some hair dye. We must change her appearance.* Eddie picked out two different kinds - brown and reddish-brown. He also picked out a travel-size hair-cutting kit.

In the checkout lane, Eddie was anxious to get through. He sized up the cashier - a lady, probably in her forties - and he prepared for scrutiny. As he moved closer, he worked himself up so much he was ready to tell the old hag off. "This is America, damn it. Mind your own business lady," he was ready to say.

The customer in front of him left, and the cashier fixed her eyes on Eddie.

He was ready.

"Good afternoon," she said. "How are you today?"

Eddie was not ready for that question. He only managed to grunt.

The lady laughed and then completed the order without giving a second thought to Eddie or his items. "Have a better day," she said, handing Eddie the receipt.

Eddie, still wound tight, managed to say, "Thanks, you too."

He was out of the supermarket without any trouble. He felt a sense of pride and accomplishment as he loaded his supplies into the trunk of his car. Optimism was increasing with every moment that passed. It was still early in the day and preparations were ahead of schedule. He had one last hurdle to jump over as far as errands were concerned. He needed to buy Marilyn some clothes to wear - women's clothes - and that purchase was going to be awkward. He bought some items for her before, but not *all* of the items a woman needs.

Eddie drove past two department stores on his way to the one located at the far end of the mall. He chose the one that was packed with customers. His activities would get lost in the crowd.

Eddie inched his way through one of the countless racks of women's clothing, not sure what to look for. He found himself looking for people who might be noticing him rather than looking for cloths. He was, as far as he could tell, the only man in that section, and he was surrounded by women, who were also, it seemed, aware of his presence.

"Can I help you?" a voice called from behind him.

Eddie whirled around. Standing behind him was a short woman, who looked to be in her thirties. He evaluated her. She was of average height with a pretty face that was covered with a little too much makeup. Her clothes bulged slightly in a few spots, but she still held an attractive figure. Lastly, Eddie noticed the nametag pinned to her full - but not too full - chest displayed her name: LINDA.

"Can I help you?" Linda repeated.

"I'm not sure. I'm not sure what I'm doing."

"Do you need to buy something for a girl?"

Eddie hesitated. "Yes. Actually, I do. For a girl. A girlfriend. *My* girlfriend."

Linda giggled. "You haven't done this before, have you?"

Eddie bought a few things for Marilyn before, but not to the extent he needed to do this time. "No. No, I haven't."

"That's okay," Linda continued. "Are you looking for anything specific?"

"She needs…Well, she just flew in and her bags got lost."

"I see. I hate when that happens. You'd be surprised how often that happens."

"Really?"

"I don't know. No, not really," Linda said with a laugh. "But I'm sure it *does* happen."

Eddie shifted from one foot to the other. "I need a lot of clothes, but I don't really know her size."

"Is she coming to join you?" Linda asked.

"What do you mean?"

"Is she coming to shop for clothes? To shop with you?"

"Oh. No. No, she's not."

"Maybe you can call her to get her sizes."

"No. It's just…I can't."

"That's okay," Linda said. "That's what I'm here for. We'll figure something out."

With Linda's help, Eddie managed to navigate the crowd and select two pairs of jeans, two t-shirts, a sweatshirt, socks and a pair of shoes. And nobody seemed to pay much attention to him. He waited while Linda added the shoes to the pile accumulating at the customer service desk. When she returned, she asked, "Is there anything else I can help you find?"

Before Eddie had a chance to respond, Linda followed his gaze to a nearby mannequin and read his mind. "Does she need some undergarments?"

"I guess I should get her some."

"Don't be shy," Linda said, patting his shoulder. "Let's see. You said she would probably wear my pant size. I wear mediums, so that'll probably fit her. How many do you think she'll need?"

"I don't know. Maybe one pack?"

"One pack?" Linda snickered. "You poor, clueless man. I doubt your girlfriend is going to be wearing granny panties." Linda grabbed Eddie's arm and pulled him over to a bin piled high with panties. "These are all medium."

Linda pawed through the pile. "These ones are cute." She held up a pair of pink, polka-dotted panties. "Does she wear this kind?"

Eddie stuttered.

"Don't play me for a fool, now," Linda teased. "I know you know."

"Yes. Those will be fine."

"How about these and some of these?" Linda asked, pulling out a few more.

"Perfect," Eddie said. "Thanks."

"Alright, then. That was the easy part. How about up top?" Linda nodded toward a nearby mannequin's breasts. "Is she bigger than that?"

Eddie hesitated, trying to pretend he was making an honest assessment and not being perverted. "I think she's about that big in the shoulders and body." He gestured to the sides of his rib cage. "But I think she's a bit bigger in the..."

"In the cups?"

"Yes."

"Okay. Good. You're thinking." Linda checked the size of the bra on the mannequin and disappeared into the lingerie section. A moment later, she returned with several bras. "The mannequin was a 'B.' This is a 'C' cup," she said, holding up the first one. "Does that look about right?"

"Maybe."

Linda held up another choice. "This one is a 'D' cup."

Eddie examined the cups. "Yes, I think so. That looks about right. It'd be better to have a bigger size than a smaller size anyway, right?"

"Yes. I agree. For your future reference, this is a thirty-six 'D.' If it fits, remember her size for next time."

Eddie laughed. *Just let me get the hell out of here,* he thought.

Eddie followed Linda through the crowd to the customer service desk where she scanned and bagged all of his items. "Thanks for all your help, Linda," Eddie said, finally feeling normal again. "I appreciate it."

"Next time get her sizes," Linda said with a wink.

Eddie scurried through the crowd on his way out, and he thought, *I'm glad that's over with. Plans are going off without a hitch!*

#

Back at the apartment, Eddie did a load of wash, packed a bag for himself and put it in the car alongside the items he purchased for Marilyn. There were only a handful of preparations left now. He sat down at his computer to draw up an escape route. He knew he wanted to drive straight through in the early morning. They should get to Canada as soon as they could. He wanted to find a place not far from the border, somewhere outside Windsor probably. According to

MapQuest, it was about a three-hour drive to Detroit, but it would be impossible to predict how long it would take to get through customs and get out of Windsor. Eddie hoped they could get somewhere more rural by noon the next day. He envisioned them eating lunch at some diner and passing out on a hotel bed - exhausted but free.

There will be less people in the country, Eddie thought, *and hopefully the hotels will be cheaper.*

He picked out a location on the map that was about four hours of driving time away, near a city named Lakeshore, Ontario. Lakeshore sounded appealing. He checked it out on *Wikipedia.* Lakeshore, Ontario had a population of about 33,000 with a mean income of about $80,000 per household.

It's Perfect, thought Eddie. *If not, there looks to be several rural towns within a manageable radius: Emeryville, St. Joachim, Pointe-Aux-Roches, Tilbury. I can take her there, find a hotel and pay for her to stay for the week. Then, I'll drive back on Monday in time for work. I can easily get there on the weekends until I can get rid of my stuff and my lease and figure out something better. The only thing left to do is to go get Marilyn and skedaddle.*

#

Eddie was sitting in his car in the dark. The engine was on and the transmission was in gear. He was staring as far as he could up the road, where the pavement met the night.

"Alright, let's do it," he said aloud, but he did not move.

Anyone in a similar situation, no matter how steadfast in their conviction, standing before such a life-changing moment has doubts. At that moment, he was not weighing the pros and cons. He was simply staring, waiting.

He imagined himself running down the road to the boiler room. He was at a dead sprint, scanning the street in front and behind him. He crossed the street, right where Bob and Sam had failed to do so, ducked into the shade of the trees and paused to scan the area before making the final dash to the boiler room. He slipped in through the broken window. He moved too hastily, and his sleeve caught on something sharp. He heard a rip. He tumbled to the cement floor in pain, but the pain was a trophy. He would be proud of his scar, of his commitment to her.

He rushed upstairs and down the hall toward the attic. He scurried up the ladder.

"Marilyn?" he called. "Marilyn, where are you? Marilyn?"

"Eddie?"

He turned on a flashlight.

"What are you doing here?" she asked, rubbing her eyes. "What time is it?"

"It's time to go. We have to go."

"What?"

"It's time to go, Marilyn. We have to go."

"Where are we going?"

"We're going to run. We have to run." He picked up a plastic crate and started to collect things Marilyn would want to keep.

"Eddie. Stop. Where are we going to go?"

"Canada. We are going to Canada, for now. We'll figure the rest out later."

Eddie reached for the blanket in Marilyn's lap. She grabbed the blanket and held on to it. "Eddie, we can't do this. I can't do this to you."

"Do what?"

"You'll be a criminal."

"I have no other choice. We have no other choice. We have to make our own way. Nobody is going to help us."

"I won't do this to you."

"You're not doing anything to me. I want to live my life with you. There's no other way. Don't you love me?"

Marilyn let go of the blanket. Eddie rolled it up and forced it into the crate.

"I do," she said. "But…"

"We can't stay like this. They'll find you. I'll lose you forever. At least this way we have a chance. If we get out of this country, maybe we can start over. We can make our own way." Eddie offered her his hand. "Now come on. Are you with me or not?"

Tears began to form in Marilyn's eyes. "I do love you, Eddie," she said, sniffling. "This has been the best time of my life. I don't want you to get mixed up like this. You can still get out."

Eddie knelt down beside her, wiped a tear from her cheek and tucked her hair behind her ears. Her big blue eyes were blurry. "I can't get out," Eddie whispered. "I can't get out, and I don't want to. I won't. I'm already in this with you. Once they find this place they're going to connect it all to me, and we'll both be headed to jail. That's what happens if we stay. But I like the other option better. We run for it. We go to Canada and try to make our own way. If we do, great. If we don't, we'll end up in jail anyway. At least if we try, we'll have each other along the way." Eddie lifted Marilyn's chin up with his forefinger until their eyes met. "What do you say? Are you with me?"

As soon as Marilyn opened her mouth, she choked on a sob.

"If you don't," Eddie continued, trying to lighten the mood, "I'm going to have to knock you out and drag you to the car. I don't want to have to do that because then they're going to add assault and kidnapping to my charges."

Marilyn smiled as Eddie wipes away her tears. Then he cupped her face in his hands, pressed his forehead to hers, and said, "I love you, and this is what we have to do."

Marilyn embraced Eddie for a moment, and she kissed him long and hard, looked him in the eye, and gave him a slight, almost undetectable nod. With that, and without another word, they began collecting her belongings, dumping them into the center of the bedding. Everything Eddie bought for her - clothes, cards, discarded food packaging - needed to disappear. Marilyn turned off the flashlight and threw it on the pile. They stood motionless in the dark, waiting for their eyes to adjust, listening to the noises of the boiler room and the night. When sight returned they worked together to bring the four corners of the blankets together to form a knapsack. Eddie motioned for Marilyn to hold the corners together. As she did so, Eddie worked one of his shoe strings loose and he used it to tie the bundle as tight as possible.

Eddie went down the ladder first. Marilyn lowered the bundle down into his arms. Eddie placed it on the floor, then helped Marilyn down the ladder. Together they carried the bundle down the hallway in the dark, feeling along the walls with their free hands for guidance.

"In here," Eddie whispered.

The room had storage shelves filled with boxes and old, stained linens. Eddie kicked a box off of a bottom shelf. They put the bundle into the vacant place and pushed it up against the wall as far as they could. He filled the rest of the shelf with linens, and Marilyn moved the box in front of it all. He pulled a large laundry cart from one corner. The sound of rusty wheels screeched in their ears. He stopped. *Fuck it.*

Eddie grabbed Marilyn's hand, and they made their way down the hallway and down the stairs. In the basement, he hoisted Marilyn out through the broken window. He overturned a five-gallon pail and, using it as a step stool, lifted himself out. The lovers made their way up the street, under the cover of darkness, feeling the fresh air wash over them on their way to Canada, to freedom.

Marilyn was silent in the passenger seat as Eddie drove for over an hour. He took an exit just past Brighton, turned into a park by a small lake and stopped the car.

"You're going to have to ride in the trunk." He waited for her to react. "I'll cover you with clothes."

She said nothing.

He grabbed her hand and squeezed. "If they search the car, it's over."

She nodded.

"I threaded a hose from the trunk to the backseat. If you get claustrophobic, breathe through the hose."

She hugged his arm and rested her head on his shoulder.

"Trying to cross the border in the middle of the night might draw too much attention," he said. "We're going to have to wait here until daylight."

She nodded again.

Eddie saw a faint glow beginning to form ahead of him - a glimpse of light rising over the horizon. He was running out of time. It was settled. The preparations were done. He was as ready as he would ever be. The only thing left to do was to get Marilyn and go.

Eddie released the brake and pulled out of the parking lot and never looked back. He was going and nothing could stop him now.

Eddie turned off of the expressway onto the Fifth Street exit. He had traveled the same way too many times to count, but this time it all seemed so foreign. He saw signs and houses and stores he'd never noticed before. In the distance, near the hospital, Eddie could see lights flashing - red and blue. As he got closer, he saw police cars everywhere. The route to the hospital was blocked off. Traffic slowed and became congested. Eddie worked the brake pedal, releasing it whenever he could move forward. A traffic officer was directing traffic down a side street, and cars were reluctantly following his orders, trying to get a look at what was going on.

Eddie waited his turn, rethinking his plan. *What can I do now? I can't get Marilyn out of there with all these cops around. Some idiot probably caused an accident at the worst possible time.*

Eddie inched his car forward, waiting in line with all the other gawkers. There were police cars surrounding the boiler room. *This can't be how it ends,* Eddie thought, pounding his fist on the steering wheel. *It can't be. It can't be!* He leaned forward in his seat, desperate to see.

Another car moved. He was next in line to go by.

Through the police barricade, he watched as two officers came out of the boiler room. The second officer stopped to hold the door open. Lights flashed. Photographers were snapping pictures. And she appeared in the doorway. Her arms restrained behind her, her head was down, and an officer was forcing her out of the door from behind.

It's over, he admitted at last. *They've got her.* He was struck by how dirty she looked - dirty and pale and scrawny. Her hair was torn and tangled, and it wasn't blond at all; it was more of a brown color that matched her eyes. *Her eyes!* They were an ordinary brown color. Her skin was blemished from acne, and her lips were thin and flat. *Those are not the lips I kissed.*

The traffic officer was at Eddie's window, blowing his whistle and yelling, although Eddie only heard muffled noises. He eased the car through the intersection as he watched the officers help her into the back seat of a nearby squad car.

It was all a dream - a goddamned dream, Eddie cursed. *A lie. It was always lie. It was never meant to be.*

Not knowing what else to do, Eddie just drove. He drove and drove, until he finally pulled the car off the road and wept.

The Rick and Rory Show

RICK (Co-host): Alright, we're back. *The Rapid* 107.7 on Grand Rapids Radio. You're listening to "The Rick and Rory Show." So, Rory?

RORY (Co-host): Yes, Rick?

RICK: We've been talking - like everyone else in West Michigan - about this Edward Waters case.

RORY: Yes.

RICK: Unless you've been living under a rock, you've heard that the DA's office officially filed the charges today.

RORY: Yes, they did.

RICK: I think this is an open and shut case. I think this guy is dirtier than dirt.

RORY: Of course you do.

RICK: What is that supposed to mean?

RORY: You assume everybody's guilty until they are proven innocent, and even then, you doubt the verdict. You're hard-headed like that.

RICK: What are you talking about?

RORY: If the courts let somebody walk and you've determined they're guilty, you preach about the how the system is a failure.

RICK: That's outrageous. That's a gross over-exaggeration.

RORY: Is it?

RICK: Okay. I tend to be more skeptical about the human race than you do.

RORY: That being said, I have a hard time being positive about this guy. I mean, it's just that there have been so many people coming forward and talking about stuff this guy was involved with. He just seems so slimy.

RICK: Wait a minute. You can't rip on me with all that pessimistic crap and then agree with me.

RORY: All I was saying is that I tend to believe in the system a little more than you. I believe they'll work it out in court. You just assume the suspect is guilty. I'm not saying Waters is guilty; I'm just saying it's hard to be objective with all the rumors circulating about him. But I recognize, until we have some real evidence, that what I'm hearing could be just that - rumors.

RICK: Let's get to some callers. We want to hear from you. What do you think about Waters now that they're officially filing charges against him? Is this guy dirtier than dirt or what? Also, if you'd encountered this Edward Waters, we'd love to hear from you too.

RORY: Alright, let's go to John in Jenison. John, what do you have for us?

JOHN (caller): Hey, guys, love the show.

RICK AND RORY: Thank you.

JOHN: I work at the Corner Bar and Grill over by the West Village apartments, where this guy was staying. I swear to God, he came in one time. It must have been in mid-June. I remember because it was friggin' hot out at the time. This guy comes in all by himself, all sweating and greasy and gross. I mean, this guy is total white trash. I know a lot of people have already said this, but he was acting all jittery and weird. He sat down and asked for a beer, so I said, "What kind? And what size?" And all that, you know? We have millions of options. He acted like I was asking him for his social security number; he was all defensive about it.

RORY: You think he's guilty, then?

JOHN: I think it's clear, like Rick said, that he's guilty of something. I mean, even if he thought that girl was homeless, who hangs around banging homeless chicks? That's got to be some kind of crime in itself.

RICK: Thanks for the call, John.

RORY: John brings up a good point. I think that is one reason I find this situation to be so weird. I've never heard of a guy - a presumably normal guy - who has an apartment and a job and a college degree, who would conceive of dating a homeless woman. That, to me, is just too weird.

RICK: That's what I'm saying. Regardless of the aiding and abetting stuff, even if he really didn't know who she was, which is a whole different issue, there's definitely something wrong with this guy.

RORY: Let's go to Wendy. She's got something really interesting.

RICK: Wendy, you're on 107.7, *The Rapid!* What's up?

WENDY (caller): Hello?

RORY: Hi, Wendy, our screener says you were attacked by Waters not too long ago. What happened?

WENDY: I'm on the Outreach Team at church, and Pastor Tom often asks the congregation - you know, if they feel called - to go up to the front to receive a blessing or something like that. What I do, as part of the Outreach Team, is look out for people who indicate they want to be blessed and encourage them to go up front or to contact Pastor Tom - that kind of thing. One Sunday, this Edward was at our church, and when Pastor Tom asked the congregation, I saw his hand go up. So I told him to go up front, but he made a big show of refusing to go, almost as if he was there to make a scene on purpose. I knew this boy was really troubled, so I thought I'd try to reach him one more time. After the service, I tried to give him one of Pastor Tom's cards, and he accosted me.

RORY: He accosted you?

WENDY: He hit me and pushed me out of his way, and then he fled.

RICK: How old are you, Wendy, if you don't mind my asking?

WENDY: I'm fifty-five years old. I'm not a grandma or anything, but I'm no spring chicken either.

RORY: Did you report this or press charges or anything?

WENDY: No. I didn't know who he was, first of all, and he left in such a hurry. It all happened so fast. I didn't even really get a good look at him, but as soon as I saw his photo on the news, I knew it was him.

RICK: Thanks, Wendy. So, Rory, how are you going to defend your man after that?

RORY: Get over it. You know I'm leaning your way this time. If Waters did that, I would definitely say that he's, as you put it, dirtier than dirt.

RICK: This guy definitely needs to be locked up for something.

RORY: Lloyd is up next. Lloyd, you're on *The Rapid!*

LLOYD (caller): I swear, kids these days don't know how to behave anymore. They don't know right from wrong. They don't even know how to be polite anymore. They just think they should have everything given to them.

RICK: That may be, Lloyd, but I think that's getting off track a little bit here. How is that related to Waters' case?

LLOYD: I, like many of your callers, had the unfortunate opportunity to run into him. I went for an interview, and he was interviewing for the same job. While we were waiting, I started trying to make small talk with him, and he blows me off. He sat there, burying his face in some girly magazine, acting like he...

RORY: Alright, Lloyd, let's not get too carried away here. What job was he applying for?

LLOYD: It was a job over at Bethany Social Services. He told me he had a degree in social work. It's no wonder he couldn't find a job in that field; he needs a social worker himself.

RICK: Thanks for the call, Lloyd.

RORY: Lloyd mentioned something I think we often forget. Waters has a degree in social work, and he's been adamant that he got into the field to help people. What does that mean?

RICK: I think he legitimately wanted to help people. I think that's why he got involved with this Norma Baker in the first place. But I think there are two possibilities here. First, it could be that Waters wanted to help people like Baker. He became frustrated because he couldn't do so within the system, so he decided to take matters into his own hands. You know how some activists get. They get upset because nobody's acting, and then they end up doing something crazy, like bombing an abortion clinic to save unborn lives. I know that's a bad example. What I mean is, maybe he was angry with the establishment and saw the opportunity to help Baker escape as some kind of strange act of humanitarian rebellion, if that makes any sense. The other possibility, in my opinion, would be that Waters legitimately thought this girl was homeless and was trying to help her, but he got too involved, too attached.

RORY: It's a very complicated case. How are the courts going to be able to decide which way is up? I really want to get to this next caller. Hi, Linda, how are you?

LINDA (caller): I'm fine. How are you guys?

RICK: Good. Linda, what do you have for us?

LINDA: I was just listening to what Rick was saying, and I think this was a calculated act of rebellion, regardless of motivations. I actually helped Waters pick out most of the items they found in his car. I won't say where, but I work at a department store. He came in looking to buy a whole bunch of clothes.

RICK: What was he looking for?

LINDA: Female clothes, mostly. It was very strange because he didn't seem to know anything about what he was looking for. He didn't know what sizes he needed or anything. And the whole time I was helping him, he was, like, scanning the store like he was afraid to be seen or something.

RORY: What did he say about the clothes? Did he say why he was buying them or who they were for?

LINDA: He told me he was buying the clothes for his girlfriend who just flew into town and her bags were lost in transfer somewhere.

RICK: Was he acting dirtier than dirt, Linda?

LINDA: He definitely knew what he was doing. Why would he need to lie to me if everything was on the up and up? Seemed pretty dirty to me.

RICK: That's a great point, Linda. Very interesting. Thanks for the call.

RORY: I don't know. He could have made up that story for any number of reasons. What if he was just uncomfortable with the situation? We all make up white lies all the time to explain why we are doing lots of stuff, not just to cover up criminal acts. Maybe he just thought that story would be easier to explain. I'll admit I've done that before.

RICK: You made up a fake story because you thought it'd be easier to explain than telling someone what you were really up to?

RORY: Yes, of course.

RICK: Do you have an example in mind?

RORY: Let's see. I like scented candles, as you know. I like to burn them while I'm working. I find it relaxing. But, let's say I'm picking one out, and I run into you, Rick. You know, the kind of meat head who would make fun of me for that for ages and ages. To avoid an awkward situation or a long explanation of what I'm doing, I might say, "My wife love's these candles. It's her birthday." It's a harmless lie, but it just helps smooth the situation over.

RICK: You need help. Do you know that? Maybe you should see one of the social workers Waters went to school with.

RORY: Alright, come on, now. You know what I mean. I think we have time for one more caller. Let's go to Sandra in East Grand Rapids. Sandra, you're on *The Rapid!*

SANDRA (caller): Hi, guys. I just wanted to respond to a previous caller. Lloyd, who called earlier, said Waters was a jerk to him. I was at that job interview as well. I actually got the job he mentioned. Lloyd is blowing that conversation way out of proportion. That guy was totally preaching at us. We were both trying to avoid him like the plague. If that makes someone a criminal, then I'm just as guilty.

RICK: That's interesting, Sandra. So what's your take on the Waters case?

SANDRA: We just don't know enough information. At this point, everything is speculation. So I don't know. Maybe he did do it; maybe he didn't. What I do know - being just out of college, like Eddie - is that our generation is having a hard enough time getting started. We don't need these people like Lloyd breathing down our necks. Whatever Lloyd's circumstances are, they have nothing to do with our generation. What I do know is my generation is trying to get started during a really tough time. It's hard enough to get a full-time job, much less really do something to impact the direction of the country.

RICK: Thanks, Linda. We're going to have to cut you off there. We are almost out of time.

RORY: Rick, I just want to make one comment in response to Linda. I think that most of us are making judgments without all the information, and I'm hopeful that the courts will be able to tease out the truth. And I think Linda's right. Lloyd has some issues with something in his life that he's wrongly projecting onto younger generations.

RICK: Alright, that's it for us. Thanks for the calls, everybody. This has been another edition of "The Rick and Rory Show" on *The Rapid* 107.7, WGGR, Grand Rapids Radio.

Exhibit Seventeen: Failure

Eddie sat on the bench on the patio in between David and Shirley and across from Sam. The sun was missing behind the expansive clouds that filled the sky, creating an unseasonably cold September day. Outside the hospital community, the deaths of Bea and Bob seemed to have slipped by unnoticed in all the excitement over the escapee, but out on that patio, their absences were palpable.

Brad had filled Eddie in with all the details. It wasn't complicated. The weekend guard found her and reported her. Marilyn would, according to Brad, "never see the light of day again, thank God."

Eddie sat on the bench in a mindless daze along with the residents.

"Did you see the Tigers' game last night, Eddie?" Sam asked.

"Yes, I did."

"Looks like they're not even going to make the playoffs this year."

"They had so much potential. Expectations were so high at the start of the season, but it turned out to be a disaster, a complete failure."

"There's always next year," Sam said. "I guess."

David said, "Bea's...flowers."

Eddie looked at David, who was pointing at the ground. There, next to the patio, in the dirt were the remains of Bea's flowers, torn and withered. There was nothing left but droopy stems and the dark-brown remnants of former petals. "That's too bad," he said. "Bea was sure she could revive them."

Shirley cleared her throat. "Eddie, did I ever tell you about the time my daddy traded the kitchen chairs to get us kids some school shoes?"

"Yes, you did."

Shirley continued regardless, "It was a hard winter that year. By spring, we didn't have any money for shoes. And you can't go to school without shoes..."

While she talked, a police car drove up and parked in front of the building. Two officers got out of the car and left it running. In honor of Bob's memory, Eddie considered pointing out the "Please turn engines off while parked in the driveway!" sign, but he didn't care enough to move.

One officer went inside, and the other officer stood at attention next to the squad car.

"There were five of us girls," Shirley continued, "and shoes are expensive. But my daddy was set on us going to school..."

The officers came out of the building and headed down the sidewalk toward the patio. Shirley stopped talking when she saw them coming.

"Do you...have a...cigarette...I can bum...from you?" asked David.

The first officer shook his head at David, walked by and stood over Eddie. "Edward Waters?"

"Yes?" Eddie replied.

"I'm going to need you to come with me to answer some questions."

Eddie stood, knees shaking. "What for?"

The other officer said, "You're under arrest for aiding and abetting a wanted criminal, Norma Baker." The officer spun Eddie around with ease and snapped handcuffs onto his wrists.

"This is America, buddy," added the first officer. "You can't hide from justice."

THE GRAND RAPIDS TIMES
Waters Found Guilty
Evidence was more than circumstantial

Edward Waters, twenty-two, was found guilty today of aiding and abetting wanted felon, Norma Baker. For as much attention the Waters' trial has received, attorneys on both sides took virtually no time at all to present their cases - less than two days. The jury took even less time to deliberate, announcing a verdict had been reached after less than an hour.

Waters plead the Fifth Amendment, and his attorneys went to great lengths to demonstrate his ignorance. However, a key piece of evidence put forth by the prosecution on the second day of proceedings sealed Waters fate. Investigators discovered that Waters' vehicle was stocked with "both men's and women's clothing and nearly two day's worth of food," authorities said. The prosecution dubbed these items "Escaping Supplies."

"The evidence against Edward Waters was more than circumstantial," said one juror. Another juror added, "For me, it was the supplies found in the car. Even if he didn't know who she was at first, I think it's clear that he intended to help her escape once he found out."

"The verdict is very disappointing," said Waters' defense attorney, Thomas DeLuder. "This is a sad day for our justice system."

Waters will await sentencing at a correctional facility outside of Grand Rapids.

In a written statement to the press, prosecutors expressed their desire to seek the maximum penalty of seven years in prison, stating, "It is our job to show people like Edward Waters how the law and the community views this kind of behavior."

Waters is expected to be sentenced later this year.

Closing Argument

To *The Grand Rapids Times* and concerned citizens:

Although I anticipate that discrepancies will arise and questions will continue to be asked, this is the most extensive and accurate account of Eddie Waters' whereabouts during that fateful summer. To return to my original question, I ask you: Is Edward Waters a criminal?

Now that you have considered Eddie Waters' version of the story, you may make your judgment. I believe reasonable agreements can be made in his defense. First, Eddie was in a fragile state of mind when he was making decisions relating to Norma Baker. He lost Bea and Bob in quick succession and was faced with the possibility of losing Norma - his Marilyn - as well.

Second, if nothing else, we should also be able to agree that public perception - influenced and perpetuated by the local media outlets - has been misguided and misinformed. Because of the media coverage and the hysteria surrounding the story, Eddie received the maximum penalty of seven years in prison for his actions, which he is currently serving. Eddie's lawyers hope to have the sentence reduced to a misdemeanor, to a penalty of less than one year in prison. Even so, I ask you, does the punishment fit the crime?

I beg of you to not only re-examine who Eddie is, but also reconsider who or what has influenced you're attitude toward the evidence. We must make every effort to be diligent, in all cases, to seek the truth. Then, and only then, can something good come from this case. If we can't recognize these errors, learn from them, and correct them, then what hope do we have for our society?

Even if Eddie was exonerated, what kind of life would he be able to lead? What kind of opportunities would be available for him? After all, who would hire him? Eddie's drive, the optimistic spirit he had as a young man, has already been destroyed. He would not be the same man he was when he graduated from college with the highest aspirations and the best of intentions. He would not be able to see Norma Baker, who will probably never again walk the earth as a free woman. Even if Eddie was able to see her, it wouldn't matter. After all, it was Marilyn whom he loved, and she was, in many ways, a figment of his imagination. To think anything else, as Eddie says, "would be a lie."

All Eddie has left is to make something of the life he has now, every day. And, with all things considered, Eddie hangs onto his dry sense of humor. "On the bright side," he tells me, "I've found steady employment. There will always be food to cook and laundry to launder in jail."

Sincerely,
Cid Goodman

About the Author

K.M. Zahrt earned a B.A. in communications from Grand Valley State University in 2007 and a M.A. in Literature from Eastern Michigan University in 2010. He won first prize for drama in the GVSU Oldenburg Writing Contest in 2006. His work has appeared in *Route Seven Magazine* and *Michiganders Post*. *Thanksgiving with Pop-Pop*, a short collection of wild tales, was published in 2013.

Odd Man Outlaw is his first novel.